THE
SIEGFRIED
CONTINGENCY

Steven H Laskin

ENRAPTURE PUBLISHING

ENRAPTURE PUBLISHING

Enrapture Publishing
www.enrapturepublishing.com

Enrapture Publishing print and digital first edition, December 2018

Edited by Allison Erin Wright

Printed in the United States of America.
ISBN 978-1-7328170-1-2 (Hardcover)
ISBN 978-1-7328170-0-5 (Paperback)
ISBN 978-1-7328170-2-9 (Kindle)
ISBN 978-1-7328170-3-6 (eBook)
ISBN 978-1-7328170-4-3 (Audiobook)

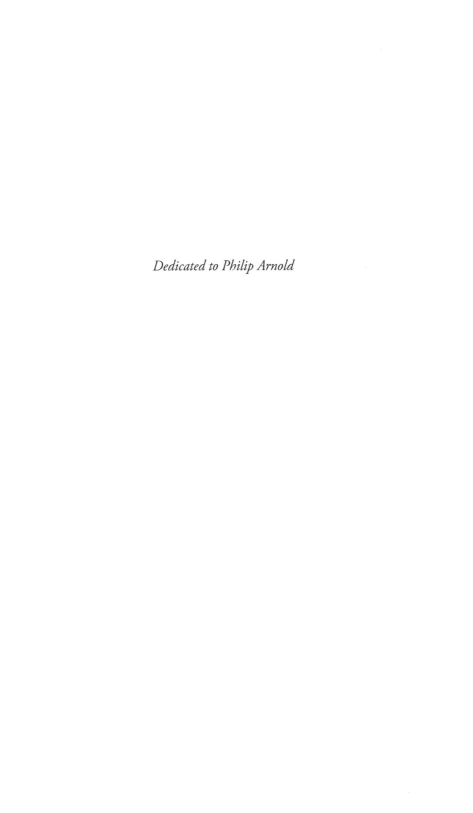

Dedicated to Philip Arnold

1

WAS RIGHT IN THE middle of trying to balance debits against credits when I first heard the noise out in the bookstore. I stopped, my pen poised over the sheet of figures I'd so laboriously transferred from a variety of sources, and listened. I didn't think then that I would look up minutes later to find myself close to death's door more prematurely than I ever could have anticipated.

In thirty-four years, I'd lived an unusually full and active life. I mean, fuller and more active than most guys my age. Four years in the US Navy, including a tour in Vietnam, plus four years sailing oil tankers in the merchant marine. I'd worked my way through college over the summers. I'd been in and out of a marriage that hadn't quite worked. I'd been employed as a professional disc jockey, a real estate salesman, a book salesman, a driver for a hematology lab, and a computer operator at several different Seattle service bureaus. And now I owned a bookstore as the sole survivor of the partnership that had established it.

But none of those things, and none of the other odd and varied moments of my life, had prepared me to face the barrel of a loaded gun with anything even remotely approaching equanimity—not even anything as sophisticated as simple fright or understandable panic. I was terror struck. A man I had never seen before was standing in front of my office desk, pointing the largest handgun I had ever seen—either in real life or on the silver screen—directly at my face.

It was roughly nine thirty in the evening. The salesclerks and the cashier had gone home at six. Judy Grenoble, my dear friend and assistant, had left sometime around eight. For the past hour and a half, I'd been sitting behind my desk working in melancholy, having received a letter that morning stating that my aunt Sophie had passed away. She'd left her estate to me, and I'd bought a plane ticket to Philadelphia earlier so I could file the necessary paperwork; I would leave the next day. While trying my best to work ahead to compensate for the time I'd be away, my mind kept wandering to the trip. I found it difficult to drag my thoughts away from it, and as a consequence, I was still sitting behind my desk when I first heard my visitor out in the store.

After several moments, hearing nothing further, I went back to the accounts and continued crunching numbers. If I were the kind of man who had it in him, I would have cursed Paul for up and dying on me, leaving me with one aspect of the business I had never really fathomed: the books. That had been Paul's end of things. And he'd maintained it very well during the two and a half years we were in business together. But for the past six months, since Paul's death, I'd felt as if the figures on the paper were gradually slipping further and further away from the reality of my financial situation.

I heard another noise in the store. Louder this time.

It was a kind of scratching sound, mixed with a sort of clicking. I wasn't sure exactly which it was, but it caused the hair on my arms to stand on end. Perhaps I was being paranoid, sitting by myself in the tiny office tucked behind the store. Maybe I was overreacting to being alone in the rear of a dark building. I don't know.

I dropped my pen and stood up, a little too quickly. My knees bumped into the desk, causing it to shake rather violently, which in turn caused my coffee cup to tip, spilling the contents across the top of the desk.

I crossed the room quickly and pulled open the door that separated the office from the bookstore in the front of the building. My heart had started pounding quietly in my chest. My breath was coming in short, rasping gasps. I could feel sweat breaking out on the palms of my hands.

Now, I wasn't a coward, and I would take it very unkindly if anyone were to suggest otherwise. But some things still frighten me. Most notably, things that can be classified in the realm of the unknown. Especially if I'm personally and immediately involved. As I was now, standing in my office in what was supposed to be an otherwise empty building, listening to strange noises coming from the room beyond. Noises that had no business being there.

I had never been particularly concerned about robbers. Very few people would take the trouble to break into a bookstore in the middle of the night to obtain a copy of the current bestseller. That reward just wasn't worth the risk. I suppose someone might risk a jail sentence for the day's proceeds, but we would take those to the night deposit box of our bank every evening just after closing, and a very official sign displayed prominently on the door stated that no money was kept on the premises after business hours.

I knew—and anyone in his or her right mind knew—that my bookstore was a very poor choice for would-be felons to practice their art. But even so, from where I got the nerve to fling open the office door with the abandon, I'll never know.

In any event, I wasn't shot. No one hit me over the head. No one thrust a leering face in front of me and told me that if I knew what was good for me, I'd freeze.

In fact, no one was there at all.

Feeling foolish, I closed the door after looking around the store carefully. Back at my desk, the coffee I'd spilled had settled into a small puddle right at the edge of the papers I'd been working on, a small amount overlapping with the sheet on which I'd transferred all the scattered figures of my financial obligations. Fortunately, only the edge of the paper was wet, leaving the ink squiggles intact. I grabbed a handful of paper towels from the dispenser over the tiny sink in the corner and mopped up the spilled coffee. Then I refilled the cup with steaming brown liquid from the coffeepot by the sink, stirred in some powdered cream, and returned to the desk and the task I'd undertaken.

At least sixty seconds went by before I heard the noise again. Louder this time. And closer.

My heart stopped beating. Or if it didn't, it felt as if it had. My hand, which had just closed over the handle of my coffee cup, froze. I looked up at the door, thinking simultaneously that I should get up and check again, that I should pick up the telephone and call the police, and that I should quickly and quietly beat a hasty retreat out the back way and come back in the morning, when it was light with other people around.

As it turned out, all those options were closed to me. In the first place, the building didn't have a rear entrance. The only way in or out was the front door, clear on the other side of the bookstore proper, which in turn was clear on the other side of the building. And in the direction from which the noise was emanating.

Second, as I learned later, the telephone line had been cut outside the building, rendering the telephone useless and my supposed call to the police a less than futile gesture.

Third, I had no need to open the door and investigate the source of the noise. The source of the noise saved me the trouble. He opened the door for me, stepped into the office, and pointed his gun right at my face.

And simple, mindless, uncontrollable terror struck me, clutching at my gut, threatening to wrench my sanity from me.

"Don't move." His voice was flat and lifeless, almost as if he were reading the words off a cue card. As if he had no personal interest in what he was saying or what was transpiring between us.

Not that I had any intention of moving. I'd never been shot before, despite several close encounters in my past, but I'd seen enough movies to fully understand how unpleasant the experience could be. If not suddenly fatal.

I opened my mouth to assure him I had no intention of moving, but nothing came out. My vocal cords were temporarily paralyzed. Instead, I shook my head back and forth to indicate I wouldn't dream of leaving our business conference before he signaled it was over. I could only hope he intended for both of us to leave in the same condition we had been in when it had started.

"You are Carl Traeger?" he asked me in the same curious, flat voice.

I suppose I could have lied to him, told him there had been some mistake and possibly even offered him some assistance in locating the party he was attempting to find. But somehow, as I stared at the very large opening in the barrel of his gun, the thought never crossed my mind.

"Yes, I am," I told him, my voice miraculously returning to me.

"You have something I want."

Now, I don't know what other people would do in similar circumstances, but I know what I did. I offered him a witty reply. "Then by all means, feel free to help yourself to it. If it's money you're after, I don't have much, but you're welcome to all of it. If you're after a good book, I could recommend—"

He took several quick steps toward me, thrusting the gun in the general vicinity of my face, and snapped, "Shut up!"

I decided that in such future circumstances, I would give witty replies a pass.

"You know what I've come for. Don't play stupid. I'm not playing games, and neither is my boss."

I had no idea what he or his superior wanted, but I'd been hoping this was just a mistake. That it was all some kind of cruel joke at my expense.

It was at this point that my terror dissolved into anger. My fear was no longer an unknown. It was standing right in front of me, pointing a very real gun at my face, and making very real threatening demands of me. And it made me angry.

I've always believed in the sanctity of the home, and by extension one's private office—which, in a real way, becomes an extension of the home for whoever occupies it. And for someone—a complete stranger—to barge in on me and wave a gun in my face…it was the ultimate violation of that sanctity. I didn't care what his reasons were or what might have motivated him to do it. I was suddenly just plain mad.

I began looking around for some way out of my predicament. Unfortunately, I didn't have any nice, heavy paperweights adorning my desk. And even if I had, I'm not sure he would have allowed me enough time to transfer my hand from my coffee cup to a weight, let alone hoist it in the air, cock it back behind my head, and fling it at him.

Then I glanced at my coffee cup. At least, as much as one can glance out of the corner of one's eye. I didn't want to give away what had just dawned on me. Flying by the seat of my pants, I decided to distract him with a lie.

"All right," I said, "I know what you've come after. But I don't keep it here."

He glared at me, his gun hand never wavering. "Where, then?"

"It's at my house."

He shook his head in disgust. "No it's not. I've already looked."

Greatly astounded, I felt a curious, sickening, sinking feeling in my stomach at the thought of this creature in my home, disturbing my memories with his very presence, violating my rooms with his touch and his look. I had a fleeting image of my belongings strewn every which way. And of Paul's things, undisturbed since his death, scattered about with callous disregard.

Getting angry all over again, I stuck to my story.

"But it is there," I protested. "It's just very well hidden."

"You're lying!" he screamed, for the first time showing any emotion at all. "There's nowhere left you could have hidden it. I searched very thoroughly."

The sick feeling became a cold, heavy lump in my stomach. It wasn't hard, now, to imagine what kind of shambles he'd left the place in. I had to stew something else, pronto.

"All right," I said, "it's not there. But it's not here either. That's the truth. It's in the safe deposit box in my bank."

His eyes narrowed. "I think you're lying again."

I glanced away from him to the pack of cigarettes on my desk just beyond my left hand. "No, I'm telling you the truth." I saw his eyes follow mine momentarily and then snap back. "You can come with me tomorrow morning when the bank opens and see for yourself."

With slow, nonstartling calculation, I moved my left hand toward the cigarettes. "Do you mind if I smoke?" I asked.

As I'd hoped, he shifted his eyes toward the movement—and his gun followed his eyes, lining up on my left hand. I knew that at best it would be a temporary diversion, and he wouldn't fall for it a second time. So as soon as his eyes shifted and the trajectory of his gun changed direction, I jerked my right arm upward, snapping my wrist to fling the contents of my coffee cup into his face.

The only objection I'd ever had to the coffeepot in my office was that it dispensed coffee about four times too hot to drink. But at that moment, I could have fallen on my knees and given thanks that such was the case—if, of course, I hadn't been otherwise occupied.

His reaction was all I could have expected. The boiling liquid hit his face, catching him by surprise. He dropped the gun as he brought both hands up to ward off the pain—a totally futile gesture, as the damage had already been done, but it was the exact gesture I'd been counting on.

I scrambled over the desk with the speed and urgency of a man whose life depended on what he did in the next several moments, for indeed it did. I must give the man credit for his self-control, because despite the terrible pain the boiling coffee must have inflicted on his face, he had not uttered even one cry to acknowledge it. As I came over the desk, his hands began to drop away from his eyes. Even without being able to see me, he knew instinctively that he was under attack.

I landed on both feet, thankful for the many hours I'd put into staying in shape at my health club, drew my right arm across my body and up under my left armpit, balled my hand into a fist, twisted my torso to the left so my right shoulder came down like a discus thrower getting ready to let fly, and snapped my arm forward like a miniature catapult, twisting my body round toward the front as I did so. My fist caught him like a sledgehammer against his exposed midriff.

I could hear the breath whistling out of his lungs as his knees began to sag. With his hands in front of his face, his eyes mirrored the shock. I grabbed his hair with my right hand and yanked his head down while lifting my right knee upward. His face connected with my knee in a bone-jarring crunch. I let go of his hair and stepped back out of his way. Very slowly, he dropped to his knees and rolled over onto the floor.

My first thought was that I'd killed him. But, looking closely, I could see his chest rising and falling in a somewhat irregular rhythm. I turned around and picked up the telephone to call the police.

That was when I discovered the line had been cut.

I knew I needed help, and professional help at that, but I wasn't sure I wanted to walk out of the store and leave him alone. Not that I was the least bit concerned he might die on my office floor—that wouldn't have bothered me in the slightest. But I was worried he might regain consciousness, get up, and simply walk out into the night. And then I might find myself in a repeat performance. That bothered me. And more than just slightly.

I compromised by picking up his gun, walking through the store and out onto the street, and crossing to the public telephone booth on the corner. I figured that with his gun in hand, I could keep watch on the door and prevent his escape, should he regain consciousness.

I deposited fifteen cents, dialed 911, and was talking to a police officer after the second ring. Very succinctly, I described my problem to him, gave him the address of the bookstore, and assured him I would wait where I was and not attempt reentry of the premises.

Two squad cars arrived at the same moment, sirens blaring and blue lights flashing. Four officers emerged, guns drawn, and split into two groups. One group converged on the entrance while the other converged on the telephone booth, where I was still standing. One of the officers thoughtfully relieved me of the pistol, which was still dangling from my hand.

I quickly explained to them that there was only one window in the rear of the building and it was securely barred. If the intruder was going to come out at all, it would have to be through the front door. They left one man outside at the door while the other three went in slowly, guns at the ready. One of them emerged a few minutes later, and I couldn't help noticing he'd holstered his weapon. I took that to mean my intruder was still unconscious.

My thought was confirmed when the officer went back to his car and radioed for an aid car. I had no trouble overhearing him explain the suspect was unconscious, breathing fairly well, and seemed in no imminent danger of transpiring. I breathed a sigh of relief that I hadn't killed him.

One of the officers took a statement from me and asked if I could come down to headquarters in the morning to check it over and sign it. I told him I'd be delighted to. I declined his offer of a lift home, explaining that I had my own car. Then, remembering what the intruder had said about searching my house, I changed my mind. A witness to the carnage he'd claimed to have committed seemed, suddenly, like a very good idea.

I gave the officer my address, and we drove in silence across the city out toward my house in Lake Washington. His partner had elected to remain at the scene and ride to the hospital with the suspect. The other two officers, I presumed, would go back out on patrol once things were wrapped up at the store.

When we got to the house, I unlocked the front door and then hesitated before opening it. I wasn't sure I was prepared to face what lay on the other side. But I felt the officer's presence behind me, so, inwardly shuddering, I pushed the door open, and we passed through.

"My God," he breathed as I turned on the lights. "It looks like someone staged a war in here."

It was a fairly good description, but I thought it a slight understatement. Unless, of course, he'd meant an atomic war. I was slightly emotionally prejudiced, though.

The place was in shambles. Furniture had been shredded, the stuffing strewn about like a fine powder over the rest of the chaos. Tables and lamps had been turned over and shattered. The wall-to-wall carpet had been torn from the floor, a good many of the floorboards ripped up. Large, ragged holes had been punched in the plaster of all four walls, the plaster and the boards beyond scattered in irregular heaps. The overhead light had been ripped out of the ceiling. It looked as if someone had used the room for demolition practice.

I felt very weak, and I would probably have fallen if the officer hadn't caught me under the arm. "You all right?" His voice sounded genuinely anxious.

I closed my eyes. "I think so. Just give me a minute."

He gave me two, and at the end of them, I opened my eyes, took a deep breath, and said, "I'll be fine. Thanks."

"What in the hell was he after?" he asked, looking around the room.

I looked also, then turned to face him. It was the first real look I'd taken at him. He was twenty-six or twenty-seven years old with a young, almost innocent face, and I wondered how he had managed to keep it looking that way in the line of work he'd chosen.

"I don't know. He didn't say. He told me I had something that belonged to him. I told him I had never seen him before and had no idea what he was talking about. He shoved his gun at me and screamed that I was a liar. I didn't know what else to do but go along with it, so I said all right, I knew what he wanted, but I didn't have it in the store. Said it was hidden in the house. He called me a liar again, informing me he'd turned the house upside down searching for it. I had no idea he'd been quite this thorough.

"At any rate, while we were talking, I saw a chance to toss my coffee at him, and I took it. While he was grabbing at his face, I jumped over the desk and punched him."

"I'd say you did a rather good job of it," the officer said.

I didn't quite know how to answer that, so I said, "I watch a lot of movies."

He had no answer for that. "I suppose we'd better look at the rest of the house."

I agreed with him. The rest of the house was much like the living room—furniture totally destroyed, walls caved in, food strewn about the kitchen in such a disgusting mess that I didn't even want to think about cleaning it up.

At the door, I said, "If you'd give me a ride back to the bookstore, I'll collect my car and find a hotel for the night. I can't face this without a good night's sleep."

He made sympathetic noises and said he'd be happy to give me a ride. On the way back, he told me his name was Randy McCutcheon. I thanked him for his trouble, and he assured me it was exactly this kind of trouble he was paid to get into. I got out of the cruiser in front of the store and thanked him again. Then, with a truly cliché parting comment, I added, "I'll see you around."

He gave me a curious half smile and said, "Sure, why not."

2

— ❦ —

I T WAS TRUE ENOUGH that I didn't know the man who had come after me. I had never seen him before. Nor had he ever seen me. Or, at least, I was reasonably certain he'd never seen me. I'd been truthful with the police when I told them that.

What bewildered me the most was *why* these people were after me.

I was sitting on the bed of a single room in one of First Avenue's cheaper hotels. Not the worst I'd ever been in, but certainly not the best. Somewhere below average, but tolerable and clean. I'd chosen it because it was close to the bookstore and because they weren't too fussy about who checked in or how little luggage they were carrying.

I tugged off my shoes and lay back on the bed. The overhead light was still on, its naked bulb casting harsh shadows around the room, but I was too tired to get up and turn it off.

The overhead light was still on when I awoke the next morning. My mouth felt like dry, dirty cotton wadding. My face itched from need of a shave, and more than anything, I wanted a shower. I'd been too tired the night before to think about such luxuries when I'd picked the hotel. Now I wished I had been a bit more particular.

Fortunately, I kept a spare razor and shaving cream along with an extra toothbrush at the store. Having paid for the room in advance, I simply walked out and closed the door behind me. On my way out of the lobby,

I glanced at a copy of the *Seattle Times*: October 15, 1975. President Ford apparently in a car accident, and the economy looking up. While that is more good than it is bad, I was never one to depend on the rabbit's foot for good luck when it obviously didn't work for the rabbit.

It was barely eight thirty. The store didn't open until nine thirty, which gave me a good half hour before my sales personnel showed up to ready things for the day's business. That was fine by me, as I wasn't all that keen on letting my employees see me looking the way I did.

I should have suspected, however, that Judy would already be there. She always beat me to work, it seemed, no matter how early I arrived. This morning was no exception.

I found her puttering around in front of the coffee maker, cleaning out yesterday's cups, filling the sugar bowl, that sort of thing. She did it for me every morning, never once complaining that it wasn't necessarily a woman's job to be doing it.

That was one of the things I really admired about Judy. She never made an issue out of the women's lib thing. Don't get me wrong. I'm all in favor of women's liberation. I'm in favor of everybody's liberation, for that matter. It would be a clear-cut case of the pot calling the kettle black if I weren't. But what I'm not in favor of are those women, or those of color, or anyone, tearing at their hair and lamenting the whole history of wrongs that have been done to them and their ancestors in the past.

In the first place, *I* wasn't guilty of performing those wrongs. And I resent any efforts to imply my guilt because I happened to be born a white, Anglo-Saxon male. Guilt by association is a poor argument at best, insidiously unjust at worst.

Anyway, Judy was about as equal a human being in my book as I ever hoped to meet. She did more work in the store than I did, and she'd been doing even more since Paul had died. As soon as I'd realized that, I'd boosted her salary until she was making more than I did. A clear case of equal pay for equal work. Or in Judy's case, more pay for more work. Nor did I find that having an employee who made more than I, the owner, an incongruous situation. She earned every penny of it. That was all that mattered to me.

I'd made a comment to her once that she didn't always have to fuss over the coffee maker. I was perfectly capable of cleaning it out and making coffee for myself. In fact, I told her, since she didn't drink coffee herself, it only seemed fair that I should do so. She told me she didn't mind; she actually enjoyed doing it, and would I please shut up and mind my own business. You can't argue with an employee like that, so I shut up.

I think it went back to Paul, who had always told her he couldn't function in the morning before he'd had at least three cups of coffee. And Judy, who'd been in love with Paul from the first day she'd come to work for us, made sure the coffee was always hot and fresh for him when we came in.

In some small way, making the coffee was a thin, tenuous link with the past—a link she was unable or unwilling to let go. I could have been jealous of that, but the thought never crossed my mind. Her love for Paul had never interfered with my life, so it was none of my business. Jealousy would have done none of us any good.

Since Paul's death, Judy and I had become very close. She'd been there when I was at my lowest point. She'd consoled me after a great loss, and for that she had my eternal gratitude. Her genuine interest in helping me through those rather sad and dark times was remarkable, especially considering I had no one else who cared.

She looked up at me when I came through the office door, and her eyes went wide with that knowing, disapproving look. Her mouth pinched tight in what looked like extreme discomfort. "Carl. You look terrible. What happened to you?"

"It's a long story," I said, "and I'll tell you all about it later. Right now, I just want to shave and brush my teeth, OK?"

"Anything you say, boss." She only called me *boss* when she was irritated with me. "The coffee's ready. Do you want me to pour you a cup?"

"That would be gratefully appreciated." Like Paul, I didn't function well without several cups of coffee.

Judy poured the coffee and set it on my desk. I was busy getting my shaving gear out of the cabinet over the sink. "Listen, Judy, could you look after things for me this morning? I have to go out for a while."

She gave me one of her disapproving looks. "You're taking an earlier flight to Philadelphia?"

She'd reminded me that I'd totally forgotten about my trip. I would have to plan a little bonus for her next paycheck. Sort of hazardous-duty pay. "No, I have to go down to the Public Safety Building and talk to the police. But Philly had completely escaped my memory!"

Her disapproving look gave way to alarm. "Why? What's wrong?"

I looked up from spreading lather on my face and saw how frightened she was. Keeping her in the dark, I decided, would do more harm than telling her what had happened. So, as I shaved, I found myself describing what had transpired in this very office only a few short hours before. Her look of alarm escalated from simple fright to terror, and then to outright horror as I told the story. Had it been a stage performance, it would have done justice to Helen Hayes. Judy had never been able to handle violence well, and it showed. I imagined she was picturing herself in my place as she heard the story, and her face was recording her reactions.

I finished the story and my shave in a dead heat.

"Carl, that's terrible. What are we to do?"

I spread toothpaste on my brush. "We don't have to worry, Judy. They have the man in custody, and I'm sure it will be a very long time before he bothers anybody again. Besides, it was me he was after, not you."

I sat at my desk after reassuring Judy that she had nothing to worry about and shooing her out into the store, then began sipping my coffee.

As usual, it was too hot to drink, but I only grinned to myself and sat back to let it cool.

While I waited, I thought about the relationship that had formed between Paul and Judy. Paul Stewart—my friend, my business partner, my roommate, my lover. And Judy Grenoble—my assistant, my friend, my right hand. It had been an improbable relationship right from the beginning. But perhaps that was what had made it so special. It had been obvious to both Paul and me that Judy had fallen head over heels in love with him halfway through her interview for the job of salesclerk. She'd brought an impressive list of qualifications with her. So impressive that I'd thought she was overqualified for the job.

But Paul, romantic that he was, took one look into her deep-brown puppy-dog eyes and told her she was hired. He never even consulted me, nor asked for my opinion, nor gave me a chance to say no. I wouldn't have, but as a full partner, I thought I should at least have had the option. I remained angry with him for all of five minutes. That was the effect Paul had on me.

Judy quickly graduated to head clerk, and, after Paul's death, I promoted her to executive assistant, with an increase in salary to go along with her new responsibilities. Not once in all the time she had worked for the bookstore did I regret the fact that Paul had decided to hire her.

I drank my coffee, checked my watch, decided against a second cup, retrieved my jacket, and left for my appointment with the police.

I had the usual difficulty of finding a place to park. Seattle needed about four times the parking space it had, and there were times when I could appreciate the argument that automobiles should be banned in favor of mass transit. Appreciate—but not agree with. I, like so many others, would have felt lost without instant personal transportation. Still, as I circled block after block trying to find an empty spot, I was almost ready to concede that mass transit was fast becoming an inevitability.

I finally found a vacant space six blocks from the Public Safety Building. With the city constantly raising the rates on parking meters, it really was no bargain to use a public space over one of the private lots, but something in me always rebelled at the thought of another man making a fortune from my predicament. I settled for parking on the street, even though it meant I might need to rush to the airport later.

It didn't take me long to find the right floor, and when I told the desk sergeant who I was and why I was there, he summoned a detective in plain clothes, who ushered me into a little cubbyhole of an office to sign the statement they'd prepared from what I'd told them the night before.

I read over the statement, assured him it was accurate and that there was nothing I wanted to add, and took the pen he offered to sign my name at the bottom. I asked him about signing a formal complaint.

"You just have, in essence," he said.

"In that case, if that's all…" Although I'd never done anything I would consider against the law, I still felt uneasy inside police stations. It was a phenomenon, I'd been told, shared by a good many perfectly innocent people.

"That's all," he said. "You'll probably have to appear as a witness if and when this joker comes to trial, but beyond that, you're free to go about your business."

"*If* he comes to trial?" I asked.

The detective sighed a very discouraged sigh. "He could die of old age before that ever happens. Court cases are stacked up so bad we may never see all of them prosecuted. Bear in mind that anyone can post bail on him."

"Oh, I see." I didn't see at all but couldn't bother pursuing it. I gulped out of fear. "Well, here's hoping."

He only nodded his head.

Back outside, I started the six-block trek back to where I'd left my car. If I'd known the detective's words meant my intruder could be on the streets again in less than twenty-four hours, I would have gotten in the car and driven it straight south to Mexico. Or maybe even Brazil.

What I did instead was head for the airport, hoping not to miss my flight to Philadelphia.

3

FTER RUSHING TO THE airport, I was relieved to make it in time for boarding. I felt mournful and frazzled throughout the flight, bereaved for Aunt Sophie and agitated by the intruder. Deeply confounded by what these crooks wanted and would destroy my house for, I wondered if Aunt Sophie's death was an awful coincidence.

The letter had arrived in the mail the day before, looking innocent like so many other envelopes with return addresses printed in the corner. It had appeared, at first glance, to be one of the many pleas for financial aid I received as a consequence of once having sent a check to Gerald Ford's campaign for the presidency. I almost threw it out unopened. But some inner instinct stopped me. I slit the envelope open with my letter knife and extracted a single sheet of heavy, cream-colored vellum.

The letter was short and to the point. My great-aunt Sophie Werner had died just a few days ago and named me sole heir to her estate. I only had to come to Philadelphia, sign the necessary papers, and make whatever arrangements I chose for the disposition of her holdings, and it would be mine. It asked only that I call ahead and make an appointment.

I must have sat at the desk for half an hour, letting the shock and grief subside enough for me to think rationally and act on the news. I had loved Aunt Sophie more than any other woman in my life, including my mother and my ex-wife. My parents had been partygoers, forever attending the never-ending round of affairs that continually blossomed along the

Philadelphia Main Line. They were way out of their league, but they pulled it off somehow, and as a consequence, they were rarely home evenings and had even less time to devote to the needs of their son.

Aunt Sophie filled the gap my parents left. My uncle Rolf died when I was still a small child, and I only had dim recollections of him. He was a very proper man who cut his meat and ate it in the very European manner, without changing his fork to his right hand. After dinner, he always took his cigar and brandy to his study to listen to the radio. It was his private sanctum, and I was not allowed to intrude.

Rolf and Sophie had two children, a boy and a girl, both of whom had died in Europe at the outbreak of the war. Sophie had escaped one step ahead of Hitler's secret police. Rolf hadn't been quite as lucky. It had taken him another three years to effect an escape, and in many ways—according to my aunt—it had left him a different man.

When I arrived in Philadelphia, I took a cab into the city from the airport, carrying my suitcase up to the fifth-floor offices of Stevens, Framp, and Davies for my appointment with Bradford L. Davies, my aunt's attorney. On first impression, he was a thin, balding, nervous little man with a perpetually worried look on his face.

I absorbed his story with complete fascination. He had not always been my aunt's attorney, having taken her on as a client only recently. That much I had known, for I had met my aunt's lifelong attorney, Justin Pederson, on several occasions before. He was a tall, rumpled sort of back-country lawyer who had been perfect for Sophie.

As Davies explained it, Pederson had died suddenly from a heart attack. Sophie had felt she needed some sort of legal counsel, so she'd contacted Mr. Davies for an appointment. He was most happy to see her. At first, Davies was under the impression that my aunt wanted to draw up her will. She explained that her will had long since been attended to and that she wanted his services as executor of her estate once she passed on, which she felt would not be in the far distant future. Assuring her that she would live to a ripe old age, he accepted her as a client. She handed over her will in a sealed envelope, along with a set of instructions she had labored over on her ancient typewriter for quite some time.

The instructions were simple enough. Among other things, they authorized him to collect the executor's fee she had written into her will, originally intended for Justin Pederson. They also instructed him to contact me upon her death and to make arrangements for me to open her safe deposit box. These things he had done.

On receiving my call, he had contacted Sophie's bank and made an appointment for that afternoon to visit the safe deposit box. We took a taxi to the bank, presented our identification and Sophie's document to the effect that I should be permitted to examine and dispose of the contents of her safe deposit box, and were escorted to the vaults.

Davies wasn't too happy about my examining the box's contents in private, but he acquiesced. Inside the drapery-enclosed booth, I opened the box and withdrew the sheaf of papers it contained. Most of them meant little to me except as keepsakes. But I found one envelope of extreme interest.

It was addressed to me in Sophie's flowing script. Beneath my name, she had written: "To be opened only in the event of my death."

For some unaccountable reason, my fingers began to tremble as I removed the letter from inside. It, like the envelope, had been written in Sophie's neat, precise hand.

Dear Carl,

I will be gone when you read this. I have arranged for this on purpose, for I couldn't bear to face you once you read what I have to tell you. May God forgive me for keeping it to myself for as long as

I have. It should have been brought out into the purifying, cleansing light so long ago.

My heart beat several times faster as I read on.

You were told, ever since you were very young, that your uncle Rolf was captured by the Nazis when he and I were attempting to escape from Germany in 1940. I beg your forgiveness, but this was a terrible lie I told you. And I cannot even tell you why I did it, except that I loved my husband despite the terrible things he did.

Your uncle Rolf was never captured by the Nazis. He was one of them, right from the beginning. I didn't understand it well enough then to know what he had involved himself with, so I kept quiet and let him go about his business. Women did that in those days, especially in the old country, and I'm afraid I was no exception. By the time I had grasped the horror of what was swallowing up my life, it was too late. Inger and little Rolf had been senselessly killed during a street riot, which nearly caused me to go insane with grief. It was this which, in later years, undoubtedly caused me to spend so much time and devotion on you.

Utterly shocked and hysteric, I continued reading.

Finally, in late 1940, I told your uncle that I wished to leave the country. As I was Jewish, this was a rather difficult thing to arrange, but Rolf was situated high in the Nazi circles, and he arranged it for me. Only at the last minute, through some incredible breakdown of communications within the groups handling my escape, did it begin to go wrong. I was almost captured by one group of the very men who were effecting my escape. However, as you know, I managed to get away. Rolf stayed behind to work with his fellow Nazis. What exactly he did, he never told me. Not even after the war when he had joined me here in the United States. He took that secret to his grave.

This much I do know. It had something to do with the book. It is an old copy of Faust in the original German. Beyond that, I know nothing of what makes it so important. But Rolf brought it with him when he fled Germany in 1944, and it was for the book that he constructed the elaborate safe I showed you in the library. Such extraordinary precautions for an old book! When I asked him why it was so valuable, he told me it was best that I did not know, that I put it from my mind and never mention it again.

Apparently, Rolf had been dying of cancer for quite some time before he discovered it. The end came so quickly that he didn't have time to pass on the book as he should have. While he lay dying, he told me that one day a man would come for the book, and he made me promise to give it to him. God forgive me, but I broke that promise. When the man came, I told him I had no knowledge of the book. At the time, I thought he believed me. But now, I feel I may have been mistaken.

Shortly after I transferred my legal affairs to the offices of Mr. Davies, Mr. Davies contacted me on behalf of a client who was interested in purchasing the copy of Faust his client was positive I had in my possession. He claimed the book was the missing volume of a specially commissioned set of great German literary works and that without the final volume, the set was incomplete as a collector's item. He offered me $20,000 for it.

Again, I denied any knowledge of the book. For some reason, deep inside me, I knew that there was evil attached to it, although I never did learn what it might be. I only knew that I did not want to let it fall into the hands my husband had intended it for.

I heard no more from Mr. Davies about his mysterious client's desire to obtain the book. Nor did I hear again from the man, Mr. John Brunner, who had originally inquired about it. I am not a clever woman, Carl, but it did not take much thinking on my part to decide that this Brunner and Mr. Davies's mysterious client were one and the same man. Do not trust Davies too highly.

My breath was coming in short, shallow gasps now. My aunt concluded,

I did not have the courage to destroy the book while I had the chance. Perhaps this was also out of respect for the love I had for your uncle. I will probably never know. But I ask you to destroy it. Destroy it immediately. There is evil connected to that book. I can feel it. Do this for me, Carl. I am an old woman who can't do it for myself because I lack the moral courage necessary. So you must do it for me.

The book is in the library safe. I have changed the combination to the date of the anniversary of your meeting that nice young man you introduced me to the summer before last.

Again, I beg of you to forgive an old woman's misplaced love and loyalty. May your life be fruitful, and may you find a love to equal the one you have lost.

Your aunt,
Sophie Werner

There were tears in my eyes as I left the cubicle, slipping the papers into my jacket pocket. I could not believe what I had just learned about my family's past. Davies wanted to know what I'd found, and I told him there was nothing but some old papers that would not interest him in the least. Then he asked me if there had been a book, or any reference to a book.

Swallowing my banging heart, I lied to him and told him no. Then he explained to me about his client who wished to secure the old copy of *Faust* he was positive my aunt had in her possession but, for some unknown reason, had been reluctant to part with. I must admit that the $20,000 was tempting, and had I not already read Sophie's letter, I probably would have done business.

Davies was carrying a briefcase. Symbol of a successful businessman, I supposed, as there was nothing he had to bring with him that necessitated it. I was carrying nothing, Sophie's papers safely tucked into the inside pocket of my sports jacket. So naturally, when we reached the street, it was Davies the snatcher went for.

We had barely stepped out of the bank when a man collided with Davies, hat pulled low over his eyes and coat collar turned high to shield the lower portion of his face, shoving Davies against me and throwing us both off balance. In a flash, he'd ripped the briefcase from Davies's hand and disappeared into the crowd. By the time we'd regained our balance, the thief was long gone.

"Do you want me to call the police?" I asked him.

"No need to bother," he said. "There was nothing of any consequence in the briefcase anyway. The most valuable thing was what was left of my lunch. What could we tell the police, anyway? Did you get a good look at him?"

I admitted I hadn't, and we left it at that.

Back at his office, I signed all the documents Davies had prepared, and he turned over the keys to Sophie's big old stone house in Bryn Mawr. I told him I would be staying there for the weekend and leave for Seattle on Sunday afternoon. It would give me a chance to go through the things in the house and decide what to do with them.

That evening, I made a reservation at Giuseppe's Italian Restaurant on Lancaster Avenue. Paul and I had eaten there once, on the visit Sophie had referred to in her letter.

All throughout the meal, I thought about the letter. I could hardly believe what she'd written. Yet I could think of no reason for her to lie to me. And the fear she must have felt had come through her words in almost palpable form. Along with the remorse for keeping it a secret for so long. It then dawned on me that perhaps this book was what the intruder had been after. If that guy was even remotely associated with my uncle, he could be extremely dangerous.

I hadn't been ready to look at the book when I'd first arrived at Sophie's house, partly because it frightened me and partly because I got too wrapped up in absorbing the memories the house brought back to me. But I resolved that once I finished dinner and went back, I would take the book from the safe and try to figure out what all the fuss was about.

I'd just stepped through the door into my aunt's house and was reaching for the hall light switch when I heard a rustling coming from the living room. Unthinking, I took two steps forward into the arch separating the living room from the hall and was just about to ask who was there when I heard a noise behind me. Then a sharp pain exploded at the base of my head, and I passed out.

When I came to, it was still dark in the house. And very quiet. I shakily got to my feet and groped the wall for the light switch. Finding it, I flicked it up and threw the hall into blinding light. I had to screw my eyelids shut for a few seconds before I could bear to look around. When I did, I almost threw up. What I could see of the house was almost identical to what had happened to my own in Seattle only yesterday.

I looked through the rest of the house quickly, and it was all the same—torn and crushed and scattered beyond belief. I went straight to the telephone and called the police. It was while I was waiting for them that I discovered the papers I'd stuck in my jacket pocket were missing.

Including the letter from my aunt.

When the police arrived, I wanted to protect my aunt's memory from the critical assessment of these strangers. So I told them only enough to make the shambles credible—about the book and the collector who had offered my aunt, through her lawyer, $20,000 for it. I told them about the snatching of Davies's briefcase, which I concluded the thief had taken under the impression the book was inside. And I told them that Davies was the only one who knew or had reason to suspect that I was staying in the house over the weekend. I suggested, gently, that they might begin their inquiries with him.

They accepted my story readily enough, had me sign a brief statement to that effect, got my Seattle address, and left me alone. The intruder must have found out about Aunt Sophie passing, and after he'd searched my house, my aunt's was next in line. While giving this notion time to sink in, I spent the rest of the weekend looking through the rubble, trying to sort out items that might still be worth saving. Fortunately, the intruder hadn't touched the paintings, probably assuming the book couldn't have been concealed within those thin sheets of canvas. None of them were by the great masters, but some were still valuable, and all of them were lovely as befit my aunt's taste in art. One especially, an Andrew Wyeth, I had always admired. I made arrangements on Saturday to have them crated and shipped to me, care of the store, in Seattle. I thought they might give the place a little extra class.

And, of course, I retrieved the book from the safe. I couldn't read German, so I found it totally incomprehensible. After glancing through it at the beginning of the weekend, I put it back and left it in the safe until I was ready to leave on Sunday afternoon. When I took it out again I packed it in my suitcase, which I never let out of my hand until I boarded the airplane back home.

4

THE HOUSE WAS BRICK, sitting well up on the side of a hill overlooking Lake Washington. The streets in that section of the city were narrow and winding, put in before automobiles had grown so large and before the time it took to get between point A and point B had grown so important. I parked my car by the curb of the narrow sidewalk and got out, letting my gaze wander up the hill to take in the grounds.

Standing with my back to the house, I could look out over the lake and watch the sailboats that inevitably dotted the water unless the weather was so foul as to make sailing impossible. At that moment, I could see three, but I knew for certain there were many others stretched along the twenty-two-mile length of the lake. It had been a long time since I'd been out sailing. I shook my head sadly at what was not to be, turned my back on the lake, and climbed the steps to the house.

I could distinctly remember buying this house with Paul. The seller was a sweet young lady who had been moving back to her hometown. She reminded me of my ex-wife, Margaret, whom I'd married even after she'd told me she was with child from another man. I was madly in love, naïve, and much too forgiving back then, and I'd thought it was the right thing to do. Getting engaged kept up appearances, quickly disguising her adulterous pregnancy to our families. Although I was deeply hurt by her infidelity, I was excited to become a father. Barely five minutes passed before I was involuntarily drafted into the armed forces.

While I served my time, my fiancée and I wrote letters to each other. In one of them, Margaret confessed she was having an ongoing affair with yet another man. I wasn't flabbergasted so much as understanding yet heartbroken. She needed a man to comfort her, and I couldn't be there. At the same time, I took note of some changes in my feelings for her, and being surrounded by other men was the impetus for that.

When I visited home for the first time, Margaret was waiting for me at the bottom of the plane's stairs. As I stepped onto the tarmac, the first words out of her mouth were "Please don't make me leave him!" Despite this, I married her anyway and stayed wed for a few more years until I couldn't bear continuing to take responsibility for a child that ultimately wasn't mine while she was still having affairs with other men. And so was I—in my mind, of course. I divorced her and moved on. In the time I'd raised Eric with her, I'd grown close to him, but I just couldn't stay.

With almost the same energy it had taken me to leave Margaret and Eric, I forced myself to confront the house that had once been my sanctuary. I'd locked the front door when I'd left before in a rather futile gesture against thieves. There was precious little left worth stealing, and I hesitated at the door, unsure if I wanted to face the ruin inside. When I finally realized it would have to be faced sometime, I opened the door and went in.

In the light of day, it looked, if anything, worse than it had when Officer McCutcheon and I had inspected the damage. I wandered listlessly through the rooms, looking at the piles of plaster and wood debris from the walls, the torn and scattered carpet from the floors, and the fragments of what had once been my furniture. Only two things had survived: the color portable television in the bedroom and a double-album recording of *Ferrante and Teicher's Greatest Hits* that Paul had given me one Christmas. The stereo was smashed beyond all recognition, and my entire record collection lay in broken fragments and scattered pieces of cardboard jackets all over the den. It looked almost as if whoever had done it had smashed the records in a fit of rage after not finding what he'd come looking for.

Looking down at the mass of shattered records, I figured there must be something of great consequence in the book Aunt Sophie had kept. Now that they had tarnished the home I'd shared with Paul and smeared my aunt's, I solemnly swore to myself that I would one day pay back whoever was responsible. Somehow. Someday.

I left the den and walked down the hall to the tiny library. It hadn't always been a library, but after one of our infrequent visits back to Philadelphia to visit my aunt, Paul had been so impressed with the library in her Bryn Mawr mansion that he'd insisted we add one to our house. I hadn't seen any reason why we shouldn't, so I'd said sure, why not. Anyway, it was Paul's money.

Paul was loaded as a result of an inheritance from his maternal grandmother. Paul's grandfather had been one of the original investors in quite a number of business ventures that had later paid off with unbelievable dividends, and by the time the old man died, he'd amassed a small fortune. Even after inheritance taxes, it had left Paul rich. And Paul, romantic fool that he'd been, had left it all to me in a will I'd never even known he'd drawn up. Shortly thereafter, I'd deposited nearly the whole estate into a separate account not to be tampered with.

I'd kept a very meager amount for the bookstore, but I hadn't touched it much. I wanted desperately to see that the bookstore could make it on its merits. A matter of pride, as any man of means will tell you. Plus, it would be foolish to pour good money after bad. I will admit that in the first couple months after Paul's death, before I began to get the hang of running the business part on my own, I compensated for several gross financial miscalculations out of my own pocket. But no more. If the store went under, it would do so on its own lack of merit as a business enterprise.

However, since Judy and I had become very close and I'd trusted her to take over as the business manager, the store had begun to show a steadily increasing profit. Not gargantuan, but in the black and showing every indication of remaining there.

When I stepped into the library Paul had been so insistent on building, I was appalled by the mess. Books had been torn from the shelves with callous lack of concern for their welfare. Many had been ripped in half, probably as a manifestation of the same frustration that had so methodically destroyed my records. Pieces of backs and pages lay everywhere among the heaps of books. But, from all outward appearances, the hiding place looked intact.

I stepped over to the middle section of shelves on the wall separating the den from the library. I knelt down and began pulling the scattered books out of the way, clearing a space on the floor until I had a bare patch in a semicircle about a foot wider than the width of the shelf section. Then I walked back across the room to the small electric heater built against the wall beneath the window. The heater itself was covered with a fancy cabinet fronted by thin, fancy steel grillwork. It formed a mock window seat, with the heater controls in a small recess on the side by the floor behind a panel that swung out when pressure was applied to the rear edge.

I think the thing that had fascinated Paul most about Aunt Sophie's library was its hiding place. Although he never admitted it, I'm rather sure the real reason Paul insisted we build a library was so he could install a hiding place of his own. Our hiding place was an exact half-scale model of the one in Aunt Sophie's house.

I opened the panel that exposed the heater's controls and reached inside. There were two controls: a circular knob that regulated the temperature and an on/off toggle switch. The upper end of the temperature range was 110 degrees Fahrenheit. The chances of anyone setting the heater that high were extremely slim, which was why we had chosen that particular thermostat.

I could feel the knob indicator pointing straight up, which meant it was still set near seventy degrees from the winter before. I snapped the toggle switch to the on position and then twisted the knob until it reached the upper extreme of 110 degrees. Then I snapped the toggle switch back off.

That was another safeguard built into the system. The toggle switch had to be in the on position *before* the thermostat was turned full on. And the thermostat had to be in the full-on position when the toggle switch was snapped off. Otherwise, the controls merely acted as heater controls. But snapped and twisted in the correct sequence, simple as it was, a complex electronic mechanism was set in motion, causing the exact effect that was occurring in front of my eyes.

The middle section of bookshelves was swinging out from the wall where I'd cleared the books away. It continued swinging until it formed a right angle with the wall, the open shelves revealing a steel door with a combination lock beside a recessed handle.

I went to the door and dialed the combination, then depressed the handle and pulled the door open. Behind it lay a very narrow room, two feet wide and six feet long. It was, in fact, a custom-designed safe. A row of shelves stretched from the top to the bottom along the left side; the right side was one large compartment from floor to ceiling. I had intended to keep the book here, but I changed my mind now that it came down to it. I didn't want a reason to come back to a house that was in shambles. Returning to the heater, I worked the controls in the opposite sequence, and the library shelves slid silently back into place.

Back downstairs in the living room, I stopped at the door and turned to look at the room once more. All during my inspection, I had been conscious of something missing from the house. When I reached for the doorknob, it finally hit me. Paul's presence was no longer there. It was as if the sacrilege done to our home had driven his spirit away from the place. I felt a great sadness as the realization descended over me.

I knew then that even if I had the house restored, I would never feel Paul in it again. So I decided then and there, with the carnage of what had once been our special place staring back at me, that I would sell it and let someone else worry about putting it back together. There was nothing left for me here any longer.

I was halfway into my car before I remembered the cat. I suppose shock and the pain of sudden loss could do that. At any rate, I hadn't given the cat one moment's thought since that joker had shoved his gun in my face the night before. And here I was, ready to go off and leave the house and everything in it behind without so much as a backward glance.

But not the cat, I decided. I would never be able to live with myself if I did that.

The cat in question was a huge orange tiger named Oliver. He and Paul had been living in a large apartment up on Capitol Hill when I met him. Paul and I had known each other briefly in college, where neither of us had suspected the other of anything other than the normally accepted standard of sexuality. That hadn't come until later.

At the time, which was halfway through my senior year at a small Midwestern college, we were both making the rounds of the available young ladies. There were always dances and events of one kind or another at which an escort of the opposite sex was deemed necessary and proper. Paul and I, if nothing else in those days, were proper.

Over the course of the semester, we became fairly good friends, double-dating on occasion, working on homework at odd moments together—things like that. Unfortunately, because we were both trying so hard to convince the world that we were exactly as it expected us to be, we never gave ourselves the chance to explore the feelings that, later, we both admitted we were experiencing.

At the end of the school year, we both left to go our separate ways, promising to keep in touch and then never finding the time to do so.

Paul went back to Seattle and tried working for his father for a while. When his father died, Paul sold the business and started living the life of the idle rich. His grandfather had already left him with a fortune, and there was no real need for him to work if he chose not to.

I went back to Philadelphia, got engaged to my ex-wife, and joined the navy. Four years later, long after divorcing her because of the incessant betrayals, I'd lost touch with Margaret and Eric. I had a brand-new discharge, and I was desperately in need of a job. My last duty station had been in Kodiak, Alaska, so I decided to settle down in Seattle. At the time, I'd quite forgotten that Seattle was Paul's hometown. In fact, I'd pretty much forgotten about Paul altogether. All I knew was that Seattle was about as far away from Philadelphia and the painful memories it held as I was likely to get.

One thing led to another, and before long I had a job driving a car for a hematology lab. It didn't pay much, but it was more than I'd gotten from the government, and it suited my needs. I lived very simply then. All I needed was a roof over my head, some clothes on my back, and a little food in the refrigerator.

And an occasional night out on the town.

It was while I was on one of my occasional nights out that I ran into Paul again. Someone tapped me on the shoulder at the bar of my favorite cocktail lounge and asked if I'd like to dance. I turned around and found myself staring up into Paul's face.

We both did a double take, then started laughing and hugging as if no one was around for miles. In fact, we were surrounded on all sides by young men like us who had come to this place in order to let their hair down and act naturally—naturally, that was, for us. Here, and in the other bars like it, we no longer had to put on the "straight" front for the benefit of our neighbors and coworkers. So, with the exception of a few mildly interested looks, no one paid any attention to our reunion.

We danced to that song and danced to a few more as the reality of our running into each other again after so long sank in. Then Paul invited me back to his place for a nightcap so we could talk over old times and catch up on the intervening years. I met Oliver as we came through the front door.

The nightcap became two, and then three, as we talked and laughed our way through nearly seven years of separate history. The evening ended with Paul and me entwined in each other's arms in his huge double bed. Oliver sat in the bedroom window box with a look of indignation pasted on his face.

Through the years, Oliver and I never developed more than a mutual tolerance for each other, although after Paul's death he did warm up to me somewhat. I suppose he figured that if he didn't, there might not be anyone else around to keep him in the style to which he was accustomed. Even though the cat and I weren't exactly bosom buddies, I couldn't just walk away and leave him.

I trudged back up the stone stairs and made a tour of the grounds. For ten minutes I called his name over and over, with no results. Either he was being obstinate, which was one of his specialties, or the noise and confusion of last night's demolition had frightened him away. Either way, I finally concluded that I was accomplishing nothing by standing there in the backyard straining my voice and my patience. Finally, regretfully, I went back to the car and left.

I had planned on going back to the bookstore and putting in a call to the real estate company from which Paul and I had bought the house. And I probably would have done just that if I hadn't noticed the car following me.

5

—❦—

AT FIRST, I COULDN'T be sure. I thought it was just my imagination. After all, there was nothing unusual about an automobile traveling in the same direction as the one in front of it. There were only so many roads to drive on and only so many places to drive to, so the odds were that once in a while, two adjacent cars would wind up heading from the same point A to the same point B at the same time.

However, after the events of the night before, I was still a trifle paranoid. So I decided to prove to myself that it was only a coincidence. At the next intersection, I turned left, then left again, then left a third time so I was heading back across the street I'd been traveling on. I went two blocks and turned right, then right again, and then right a third time, so I was now heading in the same direction on the same street where I'd started my evasive maneuvers. In other words, I drove in a square-sided figure eight. And to be perfectly sure, I went through the routine two more times.

At the end of which, the other car was still there.

There was no mistaking it. It *was* the same car, a bright-blue Lincoln Continental with a white vinyl roof. The final proof was the bumper sticker clearly visible in my rearview mirror. It read MAFIA STAFF CAR. The chances of two bright-blue Lincolns with white vinyl roofs and identical bumper stickers coming up behind me at practically the same time on the same street were too astronomical to even consider.

I looked down to my right at the book I'd decided not to stash in the safe in the house. It was the book they were after—not me. If I had any sense at all, I'd open the window, drop the book gently out onto the street, and beat a hasty retreat.

If I had any sense. It was something, in my entire life, no one had ever accused me of.

I couldn't help but think of the house and the threat on my life, and when I did, I became livid. When I thought about what they'd done to the home Paul and I had shared, it caused a sharp signal of agony to travel through my body. I wasn't going to let them get what they wanted. Not after everything they'd done, and not with something that could become dangerous the moment it landed in their hands. Why it was of such interest to them bewildered me, but I vowed to myself I would do everything in my power to keep these lawless men from ensnaring the book from me. I intended on maintaining my aunt's wishes.

I was heading west on Madison Street, and just over the hill was an on-ramp to Interstate 5 heading north. I figured, with any luck, I could lose them on the freeway and consider the consequences later. But I certainly had the deck stacked against me. They were driving a large, heavy Lincoln, and I was in a small, light Datsun 240Z. My car was fast enough, but I had no doubt that the Lincoln could keep up with it. If they caught me at the wrong moment in a one-on-one demonstration of force, my car wouldn't stand a chance.

Whoever these people were—and I still wasn't sure who had employed them—there were more of them than there were of me. The one who had threatened to blow my head off the night before was in jail, so there had to be at least two. Given the power and resources they had already demonstrated, it was reasonable to assume there were more than two.

Someone wanted the book I had, badly enough to demolish my house and threaten my life with a pistol-packing goon. There was, therefore, no reason to assume they would hesitate to shoot first and ask questions later. So if I didn't hand over the book like a good boy, it was a reasonable certainty that when they caught up with me, my lease on life would be terminated prematurely.

My car nosed up over the hill, and then I headed down toward the intersection with the freeway and the inevitable traffic light. So far, by a combination of luck and carefully controlling my speed, I'd managed to hit every green light between the intersection where I'd pulled the figure eight and the one in front of me. Now I changed my tactics. Slowing the car gradually, I hit the intersection just as the light turned red. I rolled to a stop and waited. I'd already locked both of my doors, and I didn't think they'd try to take me there; it was too public, too many other cars and drivers around.

But up on the freeway, it would be a different matter. Simple enough to stage a sideswipe that would look accidental. And if they pulled it off professionally enough, I wouldn't survive to say otherwise. My plan was to not give them that chance. But I had to make them *think* the chance existed.

My fingers played nervously on the shift knob, and I could feel sweat breaking out on my palms. As cold and calculated as I was, sitting there figuring out my moves, I felt scared deep down inside where it counted. I realized suddenly that having watched scores of movies in which chases were a critical element of the plot had not prepared me for being a participant in one. Since I'd spent many hours of my life on the road for the hematology lab, I at least knew the streets well. But this time around, I hoped my car wouldn't be filled with any red body fluid by the end of the bloodcurdling ordeal. I swallowed convulsively two or three times, afraid to blink for fear of missing the light turn green.

It turned. Coming so fast that I wasn't ready for it. I blinked twice as it sank in, then slammed the stick into first, let out the clutch, and shot into the intersection. The Lincoln was right behind me. Without signaling, I hauled the wheel to the right and squealed onto the on-ramp. The Lincoln never lost a beat. As I crested the incline, I looked into the rearview mirror. It was still behind me.

Split-second timing was the only chance I had to pull this off. As the on-ramp approached the main road, I slowed to assess the traffic I had to merge into. It was the middle of the morning, so traffic volumes were light. But there were enough cars coming for my purpose. I slowed just a little more, watching an old cream-colored Plymouth barrel up behind me off to the left. The Lincoln had no alternative but to slow as well.

At the last possible moment, I downshifted, engaged the clutch, and shot out onto the highway right in front of the oncoming Plymouth. For a moment, I thought I'd cut it too close, but the Plymouth eased back to let me in, and then I was up to highway speed and pulling away.

The Lincoln had no choice but to let the Plymouth pass and then pull in behind it. Which was exactly what I'd wanted—one car separating us. I figured it would prove frustrating to the Lincoln's driver to have me so close without being able to do anything about me. I pressed my right foot down on the accelerator and eased the speedometer up over the speed limit.

I don't know if the driver of the Plymouth thought I was playing games and decided to join in, but the Plymouth moved right back up behind me, keeping pace, and the Lincoln moved right back up behind him. We stayed like that all the way through downtown and into the slight S-curve that led into the University District.

Right at the far angle of the S-curve was a small, rarely noticed exit from the interstate, and my plan hinged on the driver of the Lincoln not knowing—or not remembering—it was there. As I saw it coming up, I began feathering the brake until I'd slowed down to about forty. Naturally, the Plymouth and the Lincoln slowed their speeds to match. In the outside lanes, cars zipped past us doing fifty-five and sixty.

I began thinking it hadn't worked, that the guy in the Plymouth was going to play the game to the end, cheating me out of a victory. Then, just about when I'd decided there wasn't enough time left, he tired of whatever game he figured I was playing and pulled out into the center lane to pass me. The Lincoln moved right in behind me, taking up the slack, and then dropped back down to forty to match my speed.

When the exit was barely a hundred yards away, I stomped on the gas, and the Datsun, shuddering from the sudden burst of speed, gathered its skirts and shot forward. I'd caught the Lincoln off guard, which was what I'd hoped to do, and it took nearly two seconds to respond. But when it did, it came at me in a rush that must have seen its speedometer pushing seventy.

At the last possible moment, as the Lincoln closed in on my rear bumper, I jerked the wheel to the right. The Datsun heaved over to the left, the unexpected shift of the center of gravity causing the springs to sag unmercifully under the additional weight. I have no way of proving it, but I'd swear the two right-hand wheels left the ground as the car swerved wildly onto the off-ramp.

As I'd hoped, I'd caught the Lincoln completely off guard for the second time. Traveling a good seventy or seventy-five, it didn't stand a chance at copying my maneuver. It shot past the off-ramp in a blur of polished blue. I saw it fly by in my side mirror as my hands fought the wheel and my foot pumped the brake in an effort to bring the Datsun back under control.

I still hadn't slowed enough to come to a stop at the foot of the hill, but a quick look told me nothing was coming in either direction along Eastlake Avenue. At the foot of the hill, I wound the wheel to the right and skidded around the corner to head back toward the city. Gradually, I brought the speed down to more or less the posted limit.

Then the trembling started. First it was just my hands, and then it took over my whole body. By the time I'd pulled over to the side of the road, I was shaking like a man in the throes of malaria. I fumbled a cigarette out of the pack in my shirt pocket and stuck it in my mouth, then found a book of matches still miraculously lying on the dashboard. It took me three to get the cigarette going. Greedily, I sucked in the smoke and began to calm down.

I sat there long enough to smoke the cigarette, and by the time I was crushing it out in the ashtray, I'd made some hasty calculations and drawn some tenuous conclusions.

The next exit the Lincoln could take was at Forty-Fifth. There was one before that, but it led east across the new floating bridge spanning Lake Washington, and once they got themselves sorted out of that highway-planning disaster, there'd be no way they could hope to catch up with me. So, if they were thinking logically, which I figured they were, they would take the exit at Forty-Fifth, cross the freeway, and double back. Or maybe they wouldn't cross the freeway, opting instead to cut through the University District until Eastlake Avenue ran into it and then come to meet me.

Their big problem was not knowing which direction I'd head once I hit Eastlake. But there were only two options, and if they chose to come down Eastlake and didn't run into me, they'd have to assume I'd gone the other way. It wouldn't mean they'd know where I'd gone, but it would narrow down the possibilities.

In either event, I decided I didn't want to be anywhere around if they showed up. Besides, as I'd already concluded, there had to be more than two of them, so there was no telling how many reinforcements they'd called in by now. I put the Datsun into gear and eased back out on the road. Several curves later, I came to a stop sign and my next major decision. I could go left up the backside of Capitol Hill, or I could go right, across the bridge that spanned the freeway, and down into the city.

I chose right and the city. There was nowhere for me to go on the hill, and in the city, I at least had the bookstore.

I'd figure out my next move once I got there. Whatever I did, I would make sure I lived up to my aunt's wishes and never let those Nazis—or whoever they were—get their hands on this book.

6

— ∞✐∿ —

DON'T KNOW WHAT I'D expected when I arrived, but somehow I'd expected something.

I parked the car six blocks from the bookstore and went the rest of the way on foot. I left the color portable television on the floor where I'd stowed it back at the house and the Ferrante and Teicher records on the passenger seat. The book was tucked tightly under my arm beneath my jacket.

I approached the store cautiously, keeping my eyes peeled for the blue Continental. I didn't see it anywhere—but then, they wouldn't have to come in the car I already knew and would recognize. From across the street, everything appeared to be normal inside the bookstore. Through the glass I could see two or three customers milling around between the displays, stooping now and then to look closer at a book on a bottom shelf, then standing back up and moving on. One of them brought a book to the sales register, and I saw Molly, the red-headed clerk, check her out. She left the store with her purchase tucked inside a new bag with the store's name, Nook & Cranny, printed boldly on the side.

I stood in the doorway of the building across the street as inconspicuously as possible until two more browsers had entered the store and departed. While I waited, I saw Judy emerge from the office in the back. Finally, I decided things were normal in the store—no one was covertly holding the occupants at gunpoint and forcing them to act normally. I crossed the street and entered.

Judy looked up as I came in, then crossed the room to meet me. "How did your trip go, Carl?"

"Nothing too eventful; I just had to go through the formalities with my aunt's estate."

"Did you visit your house?"

I frowned at her. "Yes, I wanted to see if it looked as bad in the light as it did before I left for Philly."

Her eyes were concentrating on me hard. "Did it?"

"Worse." I tried to laugh, but it came out hollow and phony. "I looked for the cat while I was there. I didn't find him, though. I suppose whoever it was last week frightened him off. I guess I'll have to go back tomorrow and look again."

"I'll help if you need me," Judy said.

"Thanks. I may take you up on that." I smiled at her. "So, how's the fort been in my absence?"

I'd slipped out of my jacket by then, and we were moving toward the office. The book was cradled in my left hand, still out of sight beneath the jacket.

"No complaints," she answered. "We didn't have any unusual run on sales, if that's what you mean. You did get two phone calls and a letter, though."

I felt a chill go up my spine, the paranoia gripping at me again. Somehow I managed to keep my voice calm. "Oh? Who from?"

She shook her head as she reached for the coffeepot and began pouring two cups. "I don't know. I didn't open the letter, and there's no information on the envelope indicating who it could be from."

I quickly ripped the envelope's seal after she handed it to me, then unfolded the single piece of paper inside and began reading its contents.

When I'd finished reading it in its entirety, I found the picture becoming clearer. The letter was from the man who was after my hide: John Brunner, president of Brunner Imports Ltd., a firm headquartered in Seattle with offices in New York, Philadelphia, Boston, Tampa, Houston, Los Angeles, and San Francisco. A very big firm. And its president wanted me very badly. Preferably dead. But not before I gave him what he knew I had in my possession. And not before I gave him the information he thought I had. This got me wondering if he had been the one who had called on the phone.

"Who were the two phone calls from, Judy?"

She stirred powdered cream into one of the cups and set it on my desk. "Two different men. I didn't recognize either voice. I told them you were out but that I expected you back before too long. Neither one would leave his name, and neither one left a message. One of them had a gravelly, unpleasant sort of voice, and he said he'd call back. What was the letter in the envelope about? Did it say where it came from?"

I sat down in the chair behind my desk, holding the letter in my hand, and stared at the telephone. "It's just an electric bill. What about the other phone call?"

"Sounded young," she said, "and pleasant. That's about all I can say about him. He didn't even say he'd call back."

I picked up my coffee and sipped at it. Too hot. I set the cup back down. "The other one say when he'd call back?"

She shook her head. "No, he didn't."

As if on cue, the telephone rang. Judy reached for it automatically. She listened for a few seconds and then said, "Just a moment, please." She covered the mouthpiece with her hand and looked at me.

"It's the guy with the gravelly, unpleasant voice," she whispered, her eyes round and worried looking.

I held out my hand, and she deposited the telephone in it, her palm still covering the mouthpiece. "He doesn't sound very happy."

"It's all right," I said, reaching for her hand. I only wished I believed it. I put the phone to my ear. "Hello. This is Carl Traeger. May I help you?"

The voice on the other end of the line was everything Judy had described it to be: harsh, raspy, and threatening. "This is your last chance, Traeger. I want the book, and I want it now."

I swallowed hard as the bottom dropped out of my stomach. "I don't know what you're talking about. Who is this, anyway?"

"You know who it is."

"Brunner? Am I right?"

"It doesn't matter who I am," he snapped viciously. "What matters is I want the book. I want it now. *And*, if you don't give it to me now, you won't live to see tomorrow. Understand?"

He'd made himself understood well enough. My hand tightened so hard on the telephone that my knuckles turned white. I heard Judy gasp off to my right, and I glanced up at her. Her right hand was drawn up to her mouth, her eyes twice as wide as before. I'd never seen anyone so frightened. The telephone was slightly away from my ear, and she must have heard every word.

"I'm afraid I can't do that, Brunner," I said.

There was a short, dry chuckle at the other end of the line. "I'm afraid I'm not leaving you that choice, Mr. Traeger. I've sent another representative to collect the book. He should be there shortly. And I warn you, either he gets the book—or else. Make no mistake about that." And the line went dead.

I hung up the phone and looked at Judy. "You heard?"

She nodded, looking too frightened to answer.

I stood up, took her hand, and pulled it down away from her face. "Hey, don't look so scared. He's bluffing." I said it with more conviction than I felt, more for her benefit than my own.

Her eyes narrowed fractionally, but she still looked terrified.

"Carl, what's going on?" Her voice came out barely above a whisper.

"Nothing you need to concern yourself with. Don't worry about it, OK?"

She stood unmoving. "What's this book he's talking about?"

It was lying on the corner of my desk, underneath my jacket where I'd set it down when we came in. I slid it out, picked it up, and held it out to her. "This one."

She reached for it tentatively, as if it had the power to snap her hand off. Her eyes squinted into a frown as she tried to read the title. Since she spoke no German that I was aware of, I didn't figure she'd have much luck. I still didn't know what it was. "What is it?" she asked me, her voice nearly back to normal.

"Judy, I don't know. Nor do I know why it's so important. I only know my aunt Sophie left it for me in a very well-guarded place with instructions to destroy it."

"But you didn't," she said, stating the obvious. She handed it back.

"I couldn't," I told her. "Not until I knew why she wanted it destroyed. Not until I knew why someone would try to steal it from me—would destroy my home and threaten my life trying to get it. I couldn't destroy it without knowing what it was. And, being surrounded by books all my life, I don't think I'd have it in me to destroy a book anyway. No—I need to find out what makes it so important."

I thought she was going to say something else, but we were interrupted by a knock on the office door. It opened just wide enough for Molly to poke her head through. "Excuse me, Mr. Traeger," she said shyly, "there's a gentleman out here who'd like to see you."

I don't know who jumped more—Judy or me. My heart started banging viciously against the interior of my rib cage. "A gentleman," I croaked. "What gentleman?"

"Me," a familiar voice said. The door swung open further, and I found myself staring into the face of the police officer Randy McCutcheon.

Molly stepped in front of him with a look of indignation on her face. "I'm sorry, Mr. Traeger. I asked the gentleman to wait—"

"It's all right, Molly," I said, holding up my hand. "Thank you. You can go on about your work now."

She looked at me suspiciously.

"Honestly, Molly, it's all right. The gentleman is an officer of the law." It was something I could forgive her for not seeing right off. He'd traded in his uniform for street clothes. Molly's look of indignation softened to one of embarrassment, and she hastily withdrew.

"Officer McCutcheon," I said, "please come in."

He stepped through the door and closed it behind him.

"Randy, please," he said. "Call me Randy. It's my day off, and I don't like being reminded."

"Randy, then," I said, holding out my hand. "It's nice to see you again."

We shook hands, and I offered him a cup of coffee. He took it with a little powdered cream, the same way I did. Stupid thing, really, but I liked him for it.

"So," I asked, "to what do we owe the pleasure?"

He sipped at his coffee, his eyes twinkling with pleasure. "Well, like I said, it's my day off, and I dropped by to see if you could recommend a good book."

It was so patently stupid that I couldn't help but laugh. Randy joined right in behind me. Pretty soon, Judy, who hadn't comprehended what was going on at all, started laughing too. Suddenly, she stopped and turned to me.

"Carl, *he's* a policeman. Tell him about the telephone call."

I could have strangled her on the spot, but I fought back my irritation, and as I thought about it, I realized I would need help. Randy was waiting for me to speak. So I told him. About the book and the telephone call, and the blue Lincoln. Judy's eyes went wide again as I mentioned the last part, but she said nothing until I'd finished. Then she said, "What about your aunt's instructions to des—"

"The rest of it is immaterial right now," I said, cutting her off. "What's important is that there's a man on his way here to collect the book. Or my head. And from the way Brunner sounded on the phone, it doesn't matter too much to him which it is. Personally, I don't think I should stick around much longer."

Randy set his cup down on the desk, nodding in agreement. "I think you're right. Listen, have you had lunch?"

I gave him a puzzled look. "No. What's that got to do with anything?"

"I haven't either," he said. "Why don't we go out and grab a bite to eat, and we can discuss your next move."

"All right." I picked up my jacket and began to slip it on. Then another thought crossed my mind. "What about the store? And the girls? Do you think they'll be safe?"

"I think so," he said, taking me by the elbow and directing me toward the door. His grip was strong and reassuring, and I allowed myself to be led. "Whoever it is seems to be interested in the book. Or you. Or both. He hasn't bothered with the store yet. Or your employees. I don't see any reason for him to change that."

We went to the door, and he opened it.

"As long as neither you nor the book is here, I think he'll leave the store alone. Too many witnesses."

"I guess you're right," I said.

As we stepped through the door, he turned to Judy and said in a very noble voice, "Don't worry, ma'am. I won't keep him out past bedtime."

I found it a very curious thing for him to say.

I had the book in my hand when we walked onto the street, so I quickly tucked it back under my arm and beneath my jacket, out of sight.

"Where do you want to eat?" Randy asked me.

I shook my head. "I don't really care. I'm not all that hungry."

"Hungry enough to eat a hamburger?"

"Yeah, sure, I guess so."

"Good." He threw his arm around my shoulder. "Listen, if you don't mind home cooking, I don't live too far from here. Up on Queen Anne. And I think it would be more private for us to talk about this." He looked over at me. "If it's all right with you."

I was still concentrating on the comforting weight of his arm across my shoulders. "Sure. That would be fine."

He lifted his arm and slapped me on the back. "Great. I think I've got a couple cold beers in the refrigerator too."

"I sure hope your wife doesn't mind you bringing someone home unexpectedly," I said feebly.

"Wife!" he said. Then he broke into laughter. "I don't have one. What made you think I did?"

"I don't know." I shrugged. "Too many television shows, I guess. The young cop and his wife struggling to make ends meet while he studies for the sergeant's exam. I just assumed."

We'd reached the corner of First Avenue. "Say," he said, "you don't happen to have a car handy, do you?"

"Couple blocks from here. Why?"

"Mine's in the shop; I took the bus downtown. If you don't mind?"

I stopped walking and turned to his face.

He stopped and looked puzzled. "What's wrong?"

"Let's get one thing straight," I said. "Stop asking me if I mind. When I mind, I'll tell you. OK?"

He smiled at me, causing his youthful face to take on an added dimension of charm and appeal. "Fine by me, Carl." He threw his arm around my shoulder and prodded me back along the street toward my car.

Fifteen minutes later, we were at the top of the hill. His place turned out to be an apartment building at the corner of Sixth Avenue West, right along the main bus line. It was a huge four-story structure of brown clapboard that someone had seen fit to jazz up by painting all the trim in iridescent yellows and oranges. His space was on the fourth floor. I parked the car across the street, and we went up in one of the most ancient elevators I'd ever ridden in.

Inside, he went straight into the kitchen to start fixing the hamburgers. I followed, perched myself on a stool in the corner, and lit a cigarette. Randy took some ground meat from the refrigerator and began shaping it into patties.

"Can I ask you one question before we get down to discussing this situation with the book?"

I looked up at him, not sure what he had in mind. "Sure. Ask away."

He looked away from me, as if having second thoughts about asking. Then he turned and stared directly at me. "Are you gay?"

His question caught me completely by surprise. So completely that I blurted out the truth before I'd had time to think about it. "Yes. I am. Why?"

He breathed a sigh of relief. "I thought so."

I had a strange feeling in my gut. "Why did you want to know?"

"No reason, really," he said. "It just makes it easier, that's all."

I didn't understand him. "Makes what easier?"

"Having you up here."

"I don't understand."

He grinned at me again. "I'm sorry. I thought you'd have guessed it by now."

I was totally perplexed. "Guessed what?"

He looked up from the hamburgers and stared at me again. "That I'm gay, too."

7

⸺ ❦ ⸺

I WAS SO TOTALLY STUNNED that I was unable to say anything—not that I had anything to say. I reached for the pack of cigarettes in my pocket only to discover that I was holding a lit one between my fingers. I puffed on it several times, crushed it out in the ashtray on the kitchen counter, and automatically reached for another one.

"You look shocked," he said, returning to work on the hamburgers.

I finished lighting the cigarette and looked across at him. "How else am I supposed to look? I mean, are you kidding? A gay cop?"

He laughed, low and pleasant, as he looked up at me. His face had taken on that innocent look again, highlighted by his curiously charming smile. But this time, there was a distinct undertone to it I couldn't quite place. Almost as if his face was trying to reveal some inner depth of knowledge but wasn't quite able to force it past the look of innocent youth.

"I suppose you thought there couldn't be such a thing as a gay cop?"

I shook my head, denying it, letting smoke flow out my mouth. "No, it's not that." Then I changed my mind. "Well, maybe in a way it is. I mean, I just never thought about it before. Good God! A gay *cop*! What do they think about *that* down at the station house?"

He laughed with open amusement. "*They* don't know about it, and I'd be just as happy if you didn't tell them. OK?"

"Hey! They won't hear a word of it from me." I drew on my cigarette once more and then crushed it out, vaguely conscious that my nerves were causing me to smoke too much. "What I don't understand is why you told me. You were taking quite a chance, weren't you?"

His hands were still busy shaping the meat into patties. He looked up again and said, "I didn't think so, or I wouldn't have done it. But I had some information on you that made me pretty confident I didn't have much to worry about."

My head came up on that one. It hadn't been all that long ago that the whole country had been up in arms over the reports of officials snooping into the lives of ordinary citizens like me—wiretapping, opening mail, things like that. And I had been one of the most indignant at the thought that invasion of privacy had spread so much like cancer through our society. "What kind of information? From where?" I felt an unbidden chill prickle my spine.

His voice was soft and concerned when he answered. "Hey, Carl. Don't worry about it. Please? My inquiries were very discreet, and no one knew what I was looking for. After the incident in your bookstore last week, after I took you back to your house, I got to thinking. Fantasizing, if you like. And I got curious. Surely you've been curious about other guys you've seen and been attracted to, haven't you?"

He didn't wait for an answer, taking for granted that my answer was yes. And he was right.

"Anyway, it was my day off today, so I did a little unofficial checking on my own. The real estate company that sold you and Paul the store. The agent who sold you and Paul the house. The credit bureau. Things like that. I checked into the circumstances of Paul's death and discovered he'd left you a considerable amount of money. Piece by piece, a picture emerged of you and Paul as lovers."

He looked at me again, his face set in a mask of pain. "I could have been wrong, I suppose, but I thought not. And I can't tell you how sorry

I am about Paul. I didn't know him, but he must have been something for you to have committed your life to him."

The phrase "guys *you've* been attracted to" kept ringing in my ears, and I couldn't shut it out. But his last comment caused the bile to rise in my throat. "How would you know? You don't know me well enough to make that kind of judgment. It's kind of a cheap come-on shot, isn't it? And it's the kind I don't appreciate."

Randy's look of pain dissolved into one of hurt. "Carl, I didn't mean it that way. I'm not a cheap person. At least, I don't think of myself as cheap. I've tried to be honest and open about this. I'm attracted to you. I admit that up front and out in the open. And I'm not ashamed of it. There's something about you…I'm not sure what it is, or if I can put it into words yet…but something about you that I sense…"

He put the hamburgers onto a small broiler pan and thrust them into the oven. "I'm not making much sense, am I?"

"I don't know," I said.

"Carl, look. I want to get to know you better. All right? I meant no disrespect to Paul, nor to your relationship. And I won't say another word if you ask me not to. I won't try to tell you that living in the past is futile, or that it probably betrays the past relationship more completely than anything else could, because I'm not sure you'd accept that anyway."

He picked up the pack of cigarettes I'd left on the counter and took one. Automatically, I pulled my lighter out of my pocket and lit it for him. As he accepted the light, our eyes met, and in that instant I knew I was attracted to him too. From that moment at the store when I'd said I'd see him around. But I'd been denying it to myself. Out of some misplaced loyalty to Paul? To a memory that was nearly perfect but was just that—a memory? I wasn't sure.

After having Paul prematurely taken away from me, I'd never obtained the closure I ultimately needed to move on. If he hadn't been diagnosed with cancer and given a fatal prognosis, we would have lived happily for many more years. Allaying my cut-short relationship would never seem right, and accepting my past would never be comforting. But perhaps I was being given a chance to see that a future was still possible, with Randy inspiriting that notion. The thought flashed through my mind that this was what Judy had meant about me letting go and finding some sort of social life again in the months after Paul's death. I hadn't understood it then. Or, more probably, hadn't wanted to understand that in looking for someone else, I wouldn't betray my love for Paul. It wasn't until his ghost had been exorcised from the house by the vandalism of Brunner's henchman that I'd been able to let the past become the past.

"Randy, I'm sorry. I shouldn't have said what I said. I shouldn't have thought what I thought. Last night when I got out of your car, I guess I…"

"I know," he said, resting his hand on my shoulder. "I could see it in your eyes. That's the real reason I knew, the reason I had enough courage to ask you."

I smiled at him, placing my hand over his and laying my head against his arm. My voice, as I looked up at his face and saw the tenderness in his eyes, was a half croak. "So, what do we do now?"

He stood there for a moment, lost in some private reverie of his own. Then, with a jerk, he pulled his arm away and turned back to the stove. "The first thing we do is eat lunch. After that, we'll talk about it. About us, if there's to be any possibility of an us."

Of course, we couldn't wait that long, and we talked about ourselves in general all through the meal. It wasn't until we'd finished and were stacking the dishes in the sink that I remembered the book and all the reasons I had to be terrified. Sex and love and the possibility of holding another warm, soft person against you were strong deterrents to remembering much else.

But I did remember, and I brought it up. We'd poured second cups of coffee and carried them into Randy's tiny living room. The coffee had been brewed from beans Randy had ground in an old-fashioned wood-and-copper grinder, and it tasted unbelievably fresh and delicious.

I told him about the letter I'd received and that John Brunner of Brunner Imports Ltd. had claimed accountability for the intruders. I picked up the book from the chair where I'd laid it with my jacket and carried it over to the couch. Randy took it from me and turned it over and over in his hands, as if the act of turning it over would cause it to reveal its secret. "So," he said, "this is what all the fuss is about?"

I set my cup down on the coffee table and lit another cigarette, mentally resolving for the fortieth time that week to cut down. "That's it. For the life of me, I can't figure out why Brunner thinks it's so valuable that he'd rob me to get it. Or turn my house upside down."

I could almost see the image of my house flash before Randy's eyes. "If it were diamonds, or drugs, or gold, or something like that, it would make some kind of sense," he said. "But a book. And in German, to boot. It doesn't make any kind of sense at all." He was flipping through the pages of close-ordered text, hunting for some subtle hint of what the book could mean. "I don't see any little pinpricks like they used to use for coded messages." He snapped the book closed and set it down on the cushion between us. "I don't see anything at all."

"I couldn't find anything either," I said. I wasn't really concentrating that hard on the book at this point, instead letting my eyes wander over the man I had decided I was going to take to bed. His hair was a soft, brownish-blond that hung down across his forehead, and I wanted to run my fingers through it. His blue eyes sparkled in the afternoon sunlight that was streaming through the small windows across the room. His body was lithe and slim and undoubtedly well muscled beneath the jeans and sports shirt he wore. I intended to find out.

But I knew, realistically, that it would have to wait. There were more pressing matters at hand. As I became conscious that Randy was talking to me again, I pushed those thoughts from my mind and said, "I'm sorry. What was it you were asking?"

Randy tilted his head, trying to comprehend what I might have been thinking about, and said, "I wanted you to tell me everything you know about this book. How you came to possess it. How Brunner became aware that you had it. How he contacted you about it. Everything. It might not tell me anything, but then again, it might. OK?"

"Sure," I said, looking into those incredible soft, blue eyes.

So I told him everything I knew, right from the beginning when I'd gotten the letter from Aunt Sophie's lawyer.

It had been a week earlier, to the day, and as I told Randy the story, I found it difficult to believe so much had happened in so short a time. After explaining most of my trip to Philly, I said, "And that's all I can tell you preceding my coming back to Seattle. But I left town relieved to know the guy who did the number on my house was at least behind bars. Maybe he'll be able to give the police—I mean you—something to go on."

Randy had sat quietly on the sofa, watching me as I told him the story. Once, he'd interrupted to refill our coffee cups. Other than that, he'd only smoked quietly and listened. Throughout my retelling, I'd not been able to take my eyes off him, and I was desperately hoping he'd ask me to spend the night. I hadn't wanted that with anyone since Paul's death, nor had I wanted *anything* quite so feverishly as I wanted to lie beneath the blankets of Randy's bed with him beside me.

Suddenly, he came alive. "I'm afraid I have some bad news for you," he said.

I got that cold, sinking feeling again—the feeling I'd been experiencing far too frequently ever since going to Philadelphia. "What is it?"

"The man in the store last week, the one we arrested. He's out."

I couldn't believe my ears. "Why? How?"

"Some fancy, high-priced lawyer came in this morning and posted bail for him. It's pretty standard. I did some checking on him, too. He's part of the firm that represents Brunner Imports. It's not proof that Brunner's involved, but I'd say it ties in nicely."

"What's to stop him from coming after me again?" I asked, suddenly frightened again. If he came after me a second time, I might not be so lucky.

"You'll be with me, for one thing," Randy said. "And in case you've forgotten, I'm an officer of the law. Not to mention that he doesn't know where you are. You're not at your house, so for all he knows, you could be anywhere."

A new thought hit me, chilling in its implications. "Unless someone followed me here."

8

H E LOOKED UP AT that, obviously not having considered it. "I don't think it's likely, but you may have a point. Wait here a minute. I'll go have a look around."

He slipped out the apartment door so quietly I barely heard him go, even though I was watching him as he left. I took the opportunity of his absence to look around his apartment. I'd learned a long time ago that I could learn much about a person by the way he lived and what he chose to surround himself with in the way of material possessions.

The overall impression was one of neatness and order. There weren't any clothes strewn around, even in the bedroom, where most people feel at ease letting their guard down. So few people ever see most people's bedrooms.

The kitchen was spotless. The only sign it had ever been used was the dishes we'd dirtied at lunch, which were neatly stacked in the sink, awaiting washing. And I had the feeling Randy wouldn't turn in for the night without seeing them safely cleaned and tucked away in their respective cupboards.

The towels in the bathroom were precisely aligned on the towel bars, and there was no evidence of a ring around the tub. For a bachelor, a sure sign of compulsive tidiness. I wasn't the neatest person alive, prone to leaving a shirt where it lay from time to time, and I wondered if I'd be able to put up with a man who folded his washcloths. But, I decided, anything was possible if you wanted it badly enough. And I wanted it. More than I'd ever thought possible.

I'd never believed in love at first sight, and I wasn't sure I believed in it any more at the moment. But I did know that on rare occasions, two people could meet and have perfect chemistry, and they could wind up living happily ever after. Rare indeed, and I had no idea if this would truly be the case with Randy and me. What I was sure of was that no man had ever excited me as Randy did—not even Paul in all the time I'd known him and lived with him. Glancing up, I asked his forgiveness for feeling that way. I got the feeling that he understood and bestowed his blessing on me.

In the living room, which was as neat and orderly as the rest of the apartment, I found what was obviously Randy's pride and joy: a component stereo system that must have cost him several thousand dollars. It was resting on the cabinet that housed his record collection. The right-hand door was slightly ajar, so I eased it open and took a look. A man's taste in music could also tell me a lot about the man.

There was a large selection of classical music, ranging from Beethoven and Brahms to Rachmaninoff and Tchaikovsky. There was one album of Chopin sonatas and Leonard Bernstein's recording of Gershwin's *Rhapsody in Blue* with the maestro at the piano. There was also an impressive selection of popular rock recordings, most by groups and artists I'd always enjoyed. A few motion-picture soundtracks and some light classics performed by Arthur Fiedler and the Boston Pops. All in all, some very nice music.

I'd always found that music had the ability to soothe away my tensions and fears, so I selected Leonard Pennario's recording of Rachmaninoff's *Rhapsody on a Theme of Paganini*. I slipped it onto the turntable, turned the volume up medium loud, and let the lilting waves of music wash over me.

That was where I was when Randy came back into the apartment. He looked from me to the stereo, then back again, a curious smile playing over his lips. "As far as I can tell, there's no one out there. You should be safe here for a few days until we can straighten all this out."

"I appreciate it," I said, then nodded toward the turntable. "I hope you don't mind. I couldn't resist."

He shook his head. "No, it's all right. It's one of my favorite recordings. And I don't think we should let it go to waste. Do you?"

"I don't think I understand," I said.

He walked toward me and held out his hand. "I think you do."

I guess I did. I took his hand and let him pull me to my feet. The lush orchestration filled the tiny room, creating a romantic backdrop for the exquisite artistry of Pennario's magic fingers. Deftly, he attacked each of the twenty-four variations, creating a tapestry of sound so much like other Rachmaninoff works yet uniquely its own, both by composer's invention and Pennario's intent.

Randy led me by the hand into his neat, orderly bedroom, and without another word he began removing my clothes. I made no move to protest, feeling the luxuriant warmth of his big, rough hands on me. It was a feeling I'd denied myself for too long, and I wanted it to go on forever.

I lay back on his bed and watched him undress. It was like watching a poem unfold in slow motion. I'd been right about his body. It was lithe and hard, the muscles of his arms and chest and legs bunching and unbunching in symmetrical rhythm as he stripped off his clothes. Then he was beside me, and I could feel the heat of him against me. It was a good feeling, which grew with the delicate crashing of the music from the living room.

We lay glistening with sweat from our exertions, the music long since subsided, when my deliciously numbed brain finally woke up and jolted me back to the reality of the present. I jumped off the bed and started across the room.

"Hey, where are you going?" Randy asked, rolling over onto his stomach. The muscles across his shoulders and back rippled provocatively as he propped himself on his elbows.

"Be right back," I called over my shoulder. I dashed into the living room, grabbed the book off the coffee table, and came back into the bedroom. Randy was still there, his long, muscular legs stretched out behind him, his toes bunched up against the pillow. I sat on the bed cross-legged, facing him, and held out the book.

"I just had an idea."

"So did I," he said, running his hand over my knee.

"Come on, Randy, be serious for a minute," I said in mild annoyance. But I left his hand where it was.

"All right," he said. "What's your idea?"

It had come to me in a blinding flash. Some kind of intuition, perhaps. The kind that came when you least expected it, when your mind was fully on something else altogether. But quietly in the background, it was working on all the bits and pieces, and, free of conscious interference from predetermined ideas, it suddenly achieved what hours of deliberate conscious effort had failed to do. Then it broke in and slammed the answer into the conscious computing mechanism of the brain.

"I think," I said, "we've been looking at this from the wrong angle. We've been supposing that what these people—Brunner and whoever else is involved—that what these people were interested in was the book." I held it up again to emphasize my point. "I mean, the literal, physical book. But what if it's not the book they're after, after all?"

Randy looked confused. "I'm not following you."

I didn't blame him. I only half believed what I suspected myself.

"What if it's not the book that all this hubbub is about, but something that's hidden in the book?"

"I already checked it for pinpricks, and there was nothing," he protested. "We've both checked it until we were blue in the face. If there were anything there, believe me, we would have found it. Unless, of course, you're suggesting invisible ink."

"No, of course not," I said. "Nothing that crude. But let me ask you this. If you were to seal a piece of paper inside a book jacket, would anyone be able to tell if he didn't already know?"

What I suspected hit Randy with a rush. He swung his legs around and sat up. "You're not thinking…"

"That's exactly what I'm thinking. But I'm not sure I should."

He took the book from me and looked closely at the jacket. Then he handed it back. "Could be. But remember, once you've done it—and if you're wrong—there's no putting it back together again."

"That's what scares me," I admitted. "What do you say?"

Now he was as excited as I was. "I say it's the only idea that makes any sense anymore. I'm for it."

I held the book in front of me for another ten seconds, thinking it through again, trying to decide. Then I announced, "Here goes." I opened the book, grabbed all the pages with my left hand and both covers with my right, and pulled in opposite directions. The book came away from its binding with a muted tearing sound. I dropped it on the bed and peered closely at the cover. It was leather on the outside and cardboard overlaid with binding paper leaves on the inside. Since the paper had already been ripped by my separation effort, I began there, peeling it away from the cardboard on the inside. It was easier than I'd anticipated. Randy sat hunched over, very close, his shoulder pressed against mine.

With the paper off, the cardboard was revealed as one continuous piece running across the front cover, the spine, and the back cover. It was creased where the book jacket folded. I had no way of knowing if that was standard bookbinding practice, but it was the arrangement on this book.

Carefully, I pried the cardboard away from the outer leather cover. I hadn't really believed we'd find anything, but it was there nonetheless. A folded piece of yellowed, brittle paper. I lifted it off the leather outer covering and held it up.

Randy breathed out a heavy sigh of release. "What do you suppose it is?"

I shook my head. I had no idea. None whatsoever. But whatever it was, it had to be what Brunner was so anxious to lay his hands on. "I suppose we'd better unfold it and find out."

"You do it," Randy said quietly. "And be careful. It looks kind of brittle."

He was as frightened of finding out the truth as I was.

I carefully pried the paper apart. It had been folded into quarters, and the second fold was more difficult than the first. But, utilizing extreme care, I finally managed to unfold it and smooth it out on the blanket. It looked like some kind of old official document.

"Do you read any German, I hope?" I asked.

"None," he said. He pointed down at the middle of the document, where someone had written in ink on the printed form. The ink was old, faded, and almost illegible. But only almost. There was still enough of it to read if one looked hard enough. "But I can read that all right."

"I know," I said. "The problem is, I'm having difficulty believing what I'm seeing."

"I know the feeling," Randy said.

I could feel gooseflesh crawling up on my arms and back. There were two names lettered in, side by side, in a neat, precise hand. Next to the names were identical dates: April 20, 1889. It looked for all the world, despite my inability to read German, like a birth certificate for a multiple birth.

"If this is true," I said, "it throws history into a cocked hat. You know what it appears to be, don't you?"

Randy nodded slowly, solemnly. "From this," he whispered, "it would appear that Adolf Hitler had a twin brother."

9

— ✑ —

"THE FIRST THING WE have to do is get this thing authenticated," Randy said.

We'd been sitting on the bed staring at it, neither of us saying a word, for the past five minutes.

"The first thing we have to do," I said, "is get dressed."

He laughed, but it was too forced, devoid of any real humor, lacking the conviction of him finding anything amusing. We got up off the bed and began gathering our clothes.

"Carl," he said. "This thing frightens me. I mean, if it's real, can you imagine…"

I nodded as I pulled my pants over my feet. "I can imagine. I've been frightened nearly a week. And until five minutes ago, I didn't even know what I was frightened of. Think how I feel now."

No comment was necessary, and he didn't make any. He just continued to dress, his face set in a grim mask of concentration. I pulled on my shoes, slipped my Budweiser T-shirt over my head, and reached for a cigarette. I lit it, passed it to Randy, and lit another for myself.

"You know," I said, thinking out loud, "if this is genuine—and I can't imagine anyone going to the trouble our Mr. Brunner has gone to if it isn't—it opens up whole new possibilities as to what really happened at the end of the war."

"Like what specifically?" Randy asked. He was sitting on the edge of the bed, tying the laces of his tennis shoes.

"Like, who was it who really died in that bunker in 1945—Adolf Hitler or his brother? I mean, history records no twin brother. So it must have been a carefully guarded secret. Right? There couldn't have been more than a handful of people who knew, or it would have leaked out somewhere along the line."

I drew in on the cigarette, mentally trying to fit the pieces of the puzzle together, hampered by not knowing what puzzle I was working on or what rules might apply. Exhaling, I walked from the bedroom into the living room. Randy followed.

"You think you could make some more coffee?" I asked. "I think better with coffee."

"Sure." He walked into the kitchen. I could hear him grinding beans in the wood-and-copper grinder.

"All right," I continued. "The first question—at least what I think is the first question—is this: Who would benefit from keeping the twin brother a secret? Hitler himself? Or the brother? Or someone else altogether?"

"I'd think it would have to be one of the two brothers," Randy called over his shoulder. "If it had been a third party, or several third parties, why would either one of the brothers have gone along with it?"

"Unless," I said, "whatever the third party planned happened to also benefit one or both of the brothers. Which means that, either way, the brothers had to be involved."

"Which leads us where?" Randy asked, walking into the room. "The coffee will be ready in a few minutes."

I shrugged, patting the cushion beside me on the sofa. "That's the problem. I don't know where it leads us. But whatever Brunner needs this document for, it's probably not anything good for society. What if he's with the Nazis and they use this to somehow seize power again? We've already seen that Brunner's men are vicious and violent, and they could effect another genocidal catastrophe if they got their hands on this document."

Randy sat down, and I draped my arm over his shoulders.

"I think, before we get carried too far with speculation," he said, "we ought to make sure the document is genuine."

"I've been giving that some thought," I told him, "and I think I know who can help us."

He turned his face toward mine, his blue eyes only inches away from mine. I couldn't resist the temptation. I leaned closer and kissed him gently, less with passion than with casual, secure friendliness.

"Who?" he asked when I leaned back.

You can't operate a bookstore for very long without running into some very interesting characters. One I'd run into about a year previous had all the credentials for the task of confirming the validity of the document Randy and I had in our possession. And he owed me a favor. He had tried, unsuccessfully, for quite some time to track down an obscure text on the rise of the European commercial class at the end of the Middle Ages. Recently, I'd finally located a copy of it for him through my contacts in New York. It had been a long, tedious search, and he'd sworn everlasting gratitude.

"A guy I know over at the University of Washington," I told him. "Owes me a favor. He's perfect. He's the head of the History Department. Knows more obscure facts about what happened—you name where—than anyone I've ever met. Even if he can't authenticate this document, he'll tell us who can."

"Do you think you can trust him?" Randy asked. "Because if this *is* genuine—if it turns out Adolf Hitler did have a twin brother nobody knows anything about—I think we're going to have to be very careful how we let the world in on the secret."

"I'm not sure why," I said, "but I think you're probably right. I don't know. I think we can trust him. I do know that before we're through, we're going to have to trust someone."

"You're right, I guess. I don't think either one of us can see the larger aspects of this well enough to decide what to do without some kind of expert guidance. You think you can get hold of him now?"

"I can try. His number ought to be in the phone book."

"Try it, then. I'll get the coffee."

His number was in the phone book, all right. I dialed it from the telephone on the small table next to the apartment door. Fourteen rings later, I accepted the fact that he wasn't there.

"No one home," I said.

Randy was walking in from the kitchen with the coffee. "You called him at home?"

"Yeah, sure. Why?"

He set the cups on the coffee table and sat down on the sofa. "Today's Tuesday, right?"

"Right," I agreed. Then, as he sat there grinning at me, my brain engaged itself, and comprehension seeped in. "You're right," I said. "He'd be at school."

I grabbed the phone book again, looked up the number for the university, and dialed. Two rings later, I was answered by a pleasant female voice who informed me she'd be happy to transfer my call to the History Department. Several moments later, another voice came on the line. Young. Male. Probably a student earning a little extra cash answering the departmental phone.

"Is there any way I can get in touch with Professor Wrenshurst?" I asked.

He asked me to wait. Half a minute later, he told me Professor Wrenshurst was in class at the moment, but he'd be happy to take a message. I gave him my name and telephone number, reading it off Randy's phone.

"Please have him call me as soon as he can," I asked. "And tell him it's extremely important."

"Yes sir," the boy assured me.

"Wrenshurst?" Randy asked as I hung up the phone. "Would that be Clive Wrenshurst?"

I sat beside him and reached for my coffee. "That's the one."

"I've heard of him; you know that? Didn't know he was teaching here. I read a book of his once on the Second World War. That is, it had something to do with the war, but I don't remember what, exactly."

I knew the book he was talking about. We stocked it at the store, partly because Wrenshurst was something of a local celebrity, but mostly because it was fascinating reading. It was called *But for the Mad Hatter*, and it postulated the theory that Germany might well have won the war if Hitler hadn't gone round the bend when he did. If, Wrenshurst suggested, Hitler had remained at the helm with no loss of his mental faculties, he would have been able to devise strategies and counterstrategies, not to mention shore up existing campaigns and plots, to withstand the Allied assault. Had he remained in vital, sane command, the outcome of the war most probably would have been very different.

When I described the book to Randy, he said, "That's right. I remember it now. I recall Wrenshurst arguing that something no one has yet been able to uncover must have triggered a sudden and severe snap in Hitler's mental processes. At that moment, he lost rational control, and Germany began its decline into ignominious defeat. I guess we can all be thankful it happened."

"I suppose," I said vaguely, not really paying attention. "But that's not our problem at the moment. Our real problem is verifying that this is a birth certificate and authenticating it. Then, if it turns out to be the genuine article, we have to decide what we're going to do about it. We can't let Brunner get ahold of it. His plans for it could be lethal and monstrous."

"It's very scary thinking about that part of it, isn't it?" Randy said. He lit a cigarette and leaned back against the sofa, his long legs stretching out beneath the coffee table. His coffee cup was balanced on his stomach, the fingers of his free hand curled around the handle.

"You know," I said, "I always thought of history as a static thing. You know what I mean? The past is past, and no amount of wishing can make it otherwise. But at least in this case, that might not be true."

Randy sipped at his coffee, thinking about it. He finished what was in the cup and set it on the table. As he leaned back against the sofa, he said, "I read somewhere that, at best, history is an educated guess. A composite generalization—or maybe *summary* is a better word—of what happened at a particular place at a particular time. All of it filtered through the mind of the historian—his prejudices, his objectives in writing the historical account, his oversights and errors, his educational lacks and weaknesses. Not to mention the multitude of facts and factors and motivations and feelings of all the people involved directly or indirectly. Factors and feelings that never become known, that go to the grave with those to whom they belong.

"The point was," he concluded, "that history is a fluid thing, open to interpretation and reevaluation as new facts and figures become available."

"That's kind of an unsettling thought," I said. "I mean, if you buy that, where does it leave you? You'd have to think everything you'd ever been taught was open to suspicion."

"I'm not sure it was meant to be quite that unsettling," he reassured me with a grin.

We talked about it for a few more minutes before the telephone rang. Randy nodded, and I stood to answer it. It was Clive Wrenshurst.

"Clive? This is Carl Traeger. I'd like to see you as soon as possible."

He asked me if anything was wrong.

"I don't know," I told him. "But I do know I don't want to discuss it over the phone. If it would be convenient, I'd like to meet you somewhere. Preferably somewhere private. I have something to show you. Something I think will interest you very much."

In his clipped, faintly Canadian accent, he asked me what it was.

Again, I explained that I really couldn't go into it over the phone. Finally, we settled on meeting at his home at seven o'clock that evening.

"You're coming with me, aren't you?" I asked Randy.

"You couldn't keep me away," he said.

10

— ❦ —

WE DROVE DOWN THE Counterbalance, heading south on Queen Anne Avenue toward Elliott Bay. The brick anonymity of apartment buildings lined both sides of the street as far down as the bottom of the hill, where apartments gave way to a collection of tiny shops and specialty stores that looked somehow peaceful and contented in the early evening shadows. It was too early for the night people to be out on the streets, and the workers from the surrounding office buildings had long since packed it up and gone home to wives, husbands, children, dinners, and discussions of the PTA, or rounds of midweek bowling if there was nothing decent on the idiot box. A few anxious knots of people waited impatiently at the bus stops that ran the length of the street, and here and there a body clomped along the sidewalk as if there might be someplace really important it had to get.

But I took these things in only peripherally. My mind was too distracted to focus on the passing scenery with more concentration than was necessary to keep from running the car off the road. It was instead projecting itself ahead to the meeting Randy and I were driving to. The meeting with Professor Wrenshurst. The meeting where we would, hopefully, learn whether the document we had found was genuine.

At the same time, my mind tended to drift back to the remainder of the afternoon following my telephone conversation with the professor. And in the free moments in between, those that didn't absolutely need it for the task of navigating, it settled on the broad-shouldered, smooth-faced young man in the seat next to me.

Now, despite what many people think, gay men and women do not tend toward amorous physical contact with any more statistical frequency than their nongay brothers and sisters. So, when we'd been left with nearly five hours to kill before leaving for our rendezvous, we'd spent it constructively, making an impressive dent in Randy's record collection, playing two-handed pinochle, and talking. About anything and everything, from politics to the state of pop music, from favorite foods to the best places we'd ever taken vacations. About the current status of the gay lib movement and whether it was feeling any backlash from the Radical Women on one hand and the Florida orange juice lady on the other.

But mostly, we talked about ourselves.

It seemed to me, at least in my own experiences before I'd settled down with Paul, that gay men often opened up to each other after sharing the same bed in strangely intimate and wonderful ways, though I'd be hard pressed for an answer as to why this should be truer for us than for men and women who share a casual exchange of lovemaking, if someone were to ask.

I suppose it had something to do with the preknowledge gays had that our liaisons were neither sanctioned nor accepted by society in the same way as heterosexual relationships. Therefore, in an attempt to extract every bit of warmth and tenderness possible from the few minutes or hours two people might have together, the emotional barriers would drop, allowing for remarkable intimacy. Sometimes, as with Randy and me, the sharing of those intimacies tended to strengthen the slender thread of relationship that had begun by the sharing of physical contact.

I'd asked him if it wasn't a rather exceptional strain being gay in that bastion of macho image that was the police force.

He'd looked thoughtful for a moment, as if carefully selecting his words—as if he didn't intend to say the first thing that popped into his mind. At length, he leaned back in his chair and tilted his head to the side, creating a picture of innocent wisdom that was to remain with me later when I searched my memory for pictures and images of him.

"At first," he said, "I thought it was going to be really difficult. You know what I mean? In such close contact with all those other men, in and out of the locker room, changing uniforms and all that. Showers coming off shift. Things like that. But I wanted to be a cop more than anything else in the world. Ever since I was a little kid. So I figured I'd give it a chance, see if I couldn't exercise a little self-control."

He lit a cigarette, pausing to blow out the match and deposit it in the ashtray. "At first it *was* difficult. But not in the way I'd thought it would be. I found myself overcompensating, trying so hard to be really macho, trying to make sure I didn't give myself away by making the wrong gestures or not laughing at all the dirty jokes. And what made that so difficult was the fact that I had suddenly, abruptly, stopped being myself.

"That went on for about three weeks. By then, I was so uncomfortable with myself, living with this creation I'd summoned to keep the witch burners at bay, that I stopped to reassess the situation."

"And what conclusion did you reach?" I asked him.

He smiled at me, that same devastating smile that had won me over at the very start. "I concluded that I was overreacting for no purpose. No one had ever suspected me before. I mean, I've never been obvious about it. So I dropped the act, settled down to being myself again, and got on about my business.

"The strange part is, a couple of the guys mentioned that I seemed to be more relaxed. One of them told me that a lot of rookies get tense after they leave the academy and hit the streets. And he told me it was nothing to be ashamed of. It had happened to him, too. I'll tell you—it was all I could do to keep from laughing out loud. I mean, if he'd known what I'd *really* been so uptight about…well?"

"I get the picture." I smiled back at him.

I began to like Randy that afternoon. I mean, *really* like him as a human being, for the way he thought and the beliefs he held. I had the feeling that the same happened for him. At least, I felt I'd like to believe that. We discovered what our similarities were and where our differences lay, and we concluded that none of those differences were insurmountable barriers to a continued friendship or whatever might lie beyond that in the future.

I was so relaxed in his presence, so mellowed by his companionship and our conversation, by the intimacy of our shared thinking and feeling, that I was almost able, for a little while, to put the reason for our being together out of my mind.

But only for a little while.

By six, as we ate a hasty meal of Randy's homemade vegetable soup with a dessert of cupcakes purchased at the local supermarket, the rosy glow of our afternoon's conversation had faded, replaced by the cold, glaring reality of the grim situation we were in.

We cut down Mercer Street to the I-5 on-ramp and headed north toward the University District. For a moment, I thought about the Lincoln Continental that had followed me onto the freeway before, but I quickly shook it out of my mind and went back to concentrating on my driving.

Wrenshurst lived in the Montlake section of the University District, not far from the northern periphery of the arboretum and within walking distance of the new Evergreen Point floating bridge, which spanned Lake Washington. We made it with five minutes to spare after only two wrong turns and ten minutes of being completely lost.

The house itself was a modest little stone-and-mortar number sparsely hung with ivy, with a Ford sedan of three or four years vintage squatting in the drive. What we could see of the yard in the light from the lamppost at the end of the front walk looked well manicured, if not overly large. The walk led from the drive along the front of the house to about the middle, then made an abrupt right-hand turn.

It was only after we'd made the turn that I could see the relationship of the front door to the house. It was inside a covered portico that opened out sideways instead of to the front. This required people entering the house to turn ninety degrees to the right for a second time, bringing them a full one hundred eighty degrees from their original starting direction up the walk.

Which meant that once you'd entered the portico, you could no longer see the drive, or the car, or the front lawn. Or anything. Very effective for preserving privacy.

Wrenshurst answered the doorbell with prompt efficiency, practically bowing us into the entrance hall. He was a dapper little man in his late fifties, his hair almost all turned to gray. His moustache, which was as neatly trimmed as his front lawn, was more near what I suspect his original hair color to have been, but it, too, had a few gray strands protruding.

He was wearing a pair of gray flannel slacks, and his feet were encased in bedroom slippers. A thin blue cardigan covered his blue paisley sports shirt. He led us into his modest living room and insisted on pouring a brandy for each of us before getting down to business.

Once we were all comfortably seated, brandy in hand, he said, "Now then, what was it you wanted to show me?"

I explained to him that Randy was a friend of mine who happened to be a member of the Seattle Police. That caused his right eyebrow to curl upward, but he made no comment. So I opened the book I'd brought with me and extracted the document.

"I want to explain to you before you see this," I said, "that there are some people who seem to be rather desperate to get their hands on it. Desperate enough to destroy my house searching for it. Desperate enough to hold me at gunpoint in their attempts to take it away from me. Desperate enough"—I thought of Brunner's threats—"to possibly kill in order to have it.

"I mention this because there could conceivably be some danger to you just in your knowing what this piece of paper contains. So, if you'd rather, we will get up now and leave, thereby reducing whatever risk we may be placing you in."

I didn't know why my sudden attack of conscience hit me then when it should have visited me at the very moment I'd first considered calling Wrenshurst. However, it was somewhat a moot point. The way Wrenshurst's eyebrows were jerking up and down, I could see that I had elicited such curiosity in him that nothing short of holocaust could have prevented him from wanting to see the paper.

"All right, then," I said, having given him the unsnatched opportunity to call off our meeting. "I'd like you to take a look at this and tell me, if you can, if it's authentic." I handed him the paper and sipped my brandy as he looked at it.

His first glance caused his eyebrows to shoot up to the middle of his forehead and look tight, unmoving. Then he began a careful scrutiny of the document, turning it over and over in his hands, holding it close to the small table lamp by his side and peering at it as if trying to read something on the other side. At length, his eyebrows relaxed, and he looked back at us.

"As far as I can tell," he said in a curious, hushed voice, "this is a genuine birth certificate of the type issued at the time. The watermark on the paper is certainly genuine. It both looks and feels old enough. In every way that I can determine, it is genuine. Of course, a more thorough examination by experts could tell you with absolute certainty. But I'd stake my reputation on it being the real thing."

I was conscious of an icy feeling lumbering up my spine and settling between my shoulder blades. Then I went cold all over. Across the room, I could see Randy's head drawing down into his shoulders in an instinctive and involuntary reflex toward self-protection. Before, it had been only a startling theory, a possibility to cause one's imagination to take flight. But now, with the testimony of an expert witness, it seemed to be almost certainly the truth.

"Of course," Wrenshurst went on, "the fact that the document—the actual piece of paper—is genuine in no way proves the validity of the information it contains."

What had been the beginnings of very justifiable fear turned into confusion. "I don't understand. I thought you said—"

"That the document was genuine," Wrenshurst said. "Only the document. But anyone, at the time, could have obtained such a document in one way or another and filled in anything he chose. What reason one would have for filling in this particular information if it weren't true, I have no way of even guessing. But it *could* be false information. There's no getting around that."

I thought about that for a moment and then said, "If you were asked to render an opinion, what would you say?"

I hadn't noticed it before then, but his body was very straight and very rigid, and his hands were trembling slightly.

"There were rumors shortly after the war," he told us, "to the effect that the man who died in the bunker was not Adolf Hitler but a double of some kind. That Hitler had survived the war and was in hiding somewhere, still in charge, still directing the operation and making preparations for the reemergence of the Nazi Party. A lot of research was done, many studies made, and the final outcome of it all was the general consensus that the man who had died at Eva Braun's side was actually Adolf Hitler.

"But there were some who never believed the evidence. A small handful of experts went right on believing Hitler lived, that he was hiding out somewhere, just waiting for the right moment to make his next bid. I never took that minority viewpoint seriously. Until now."

My breath caught in my throat. "You mean…"

"I mean," he said, "that in my opinion, this is more than likely the genuine article."

None of us said anything. We just sat there looking stupid, trying to let the reality—the enormity—of it sink in. The room, in the muted light from the lamp by Wrenshurst's chair, took on a hazy, unfocused appearance, as if we were suddenly underwater or in the midst of a crazy, illogical dream.

I was about to ask him if there was anyone we could see or anywhere we could go to find conclusive proof when the back of the house erupted in a crash of wood and shattering glass.

11

— ✦ —

"W E'VE BEEN FOLLOWED!" RANDY cried as he rolled off the sofa onto the floor. "Get down. Fast!"

I didn't waste any time trying to understand what was happening. The urgency in Randy's voice and the sinking feeling in my gut were enough to mobilize me. I dropped off the sofa onto the floor, wishing I could drop all the way through it and disappear.

Not so the professor. He sat stiffly upright as though he'd been galvanized, his eyes wide open with fright, his mouth hanging slackly open.

I started to rise, hoping I could get across the few feet that separated us and drag him down behind cover, but I was too late. It all happened too fast, and the professor never knew what hit him.

From the back of the house, I could hear feet crunching on broken glass, but before I could register that completely, the air was rent by the sharp crack of a pistol firing. I was up on one knee reaching toward Wrenshurst when his face exploded in a sickening confusion of blood and bone matter that fouled the coffee table in front of him as he toppled over. What was left of his head bounced off the table with a dull thud, and he slid unspectacularly onto the floor, the document still clutched in his right hand.

In that fleeting, stomach-churning moment, Randy had reached beneath his jacket and jerked out his police revolver from a belt holster

I hadn't even known he'd been wearing. His right hand came up in a blurred, sleek movement, the gun firing once before his arm had time to stop. There was a scream of pain from across the room. Foolishly, I lifted my head to see what was happening, just in time to watch Wrenshurst's assailant clutching at his forehead as he sank to his knees and disappeared behind the sofa.

"Get down!" Randy snapped at me. "There'll be more."

I was about to protest, now totally unsure of what was going on around me, totally unprepared for this sort of thing in the quiet, humdrum life I'd led up to my aunt's death, when a flash of movement behind me and to the left caught my attention. I jerked my head sideways to see what it was—two bulky figures pushing their way through the front door.

"Randy, behind you!" I screamed.

He was already moving. Lurching sideways, he tucked his right knee under him, twisted his left shoulder toward the right, and rolled to the side, taking the impact on his left shoulder. Splinters of wood and carpet exploded off the floor in the spot he'd just vacated.

As he came up out of his roll in a graceful, fluid motion, his revolver spit twice before he was on his feet. The first intruder toppled forward, his gun flying out in front of him as he grabbed his right arm with his left hand. The second intruder, now hampered by the bulk of his colleague in front of him, jerked backward and disappeared into the blackness outside.

Randy grabbed the fallen handgun and thrust it into my hand. "You may need that," he said abruptly. He was already moving across the floor toward the front door. He slammed it shut and threw the deadbolt, then quickly jumped aside as two shots rang out and two neat holes appeared in the wood, splinters flying in all directions. I felt very uneasy to have the gun. I had never killed anyone. Deep inside, I was desperately hoping I would never have to use it.

Without waiting to see if the door would hold, Randy raced across the room toward the kitchen. The assailant who'd shot Wrenshurst was lying half-in and half-out of the room beyond, the swinging door half-open, trapped against his fallen body. Randy, his revolver pointing up and held back against his right shoulder, took a deep breath and then shoved the door fully open while dropping his right arm out straight in front of him. I thought surely another exchange of gunfire was inevitable, but only silence assailed my ears. Randy grabbed the dead man by the belt and dragged him into the room, leaving him stretched across the swinging door to effectively block it.

Then footsteps approached us, the stomping of shoes against the floor growing louder and faster. In no way did I feel prepared to shoot anyone, but I had no choice. At this point it was kill or be killed. At what sounded like the final footstep before its source would come into my field of vision, I tightened my grip on the gun and secured my finger around the trigger, ready to pull despite my every instinct screaming that it was wrong. The intruder burst into the room, but before I had time to think, he was shot and went tumbling down.

"Randy, was that you?" I asked, thoroughly relieved that I didn't have to pull the trigger and optimistic that I never would.

"Yes. I was primed and prepared to shoot first," he said with no qualm or apprehension.

I thought to close the entrance from the kitchen when Randy's common sense beat me to the punch.

"There's no point in locking the kitchen door," he said. "The window is shattered." He gestured toward the telephone on the small table against the wall. "See if that thing's working, and if it is, call the police."

"But you're the—"

"And I need help," he said. "I don't know how many of them are out there, or where they are, or what they plan to do next. I only know they're pretty desperate to get their hands on that piece of paper your professor is holding."

He moved into position near the front door, but well enough away so that he wasn't in a direct line of fire and could keep an eye on the door to the kitchen. Fortunately for us, the heavy drapes over the windows were drawn so no one could see in. On the other side of the ledger, however, they also prevented us from looking out and observing what the opposition was up to.

"Don't argue with me," Randy called across the room. "Just make the call. And stay down. They might try a shot through the windows even though they can't see anything."

Less than a minute had elapsed since the first shot had brought Wrenshurst's body to the floor. I snatched the receiver off the telephone and dialed 911. When the connection was completed by an emergency operator after two rings, I was hit by a sudden burst of inspiration from the many hours of television I'd consumed since I'd been a kid. "Officer needs help," I said into the phone, keeping my voice as calm as I could manage under the circumstances. "Officer Randolph McCutcheon is standing across the room at this moment with his revolver drawn. Three men are dead, one severely wounded. The house is surrounded by men with weapons, number unknown. This is no joke; we need help, and we need it fast." I gave him the address.

He maintained a calm, professional approach to all this, not interrupting me once. "Please hurry," I said. "The call has already gone out," he assured me. Then, as if to emphasize my urgency, the front window exploded in a shower of flying glass that forced the drapes inward like a slow-motion tidal wave. I felt something tug at my sleeve, and a split second later, a stinging sensation lanced across my arm. "Hurry!" I screamed, then jammed the receiver back into its cradle and dropped to the floor. Just as I did, two more shots rang out, and two more holes penetrated the drapes.

"I told you to stay down," Randy snarled at me.

"Sorry."

"You all right?"

I looked down at the tear in my sleeve. Peeling the rent fabric away, I caught sight of blood running from a jagged, shallow groove in my skin. "I think I'll live." I pulled a clean handkerchief from my jacket pocket and stuffed it through the tear over the wound, holding it in place with my right hand.

Off in the distance, the sound of sirens cut the air in one of the most welcome sounds I had heard in my entire life. Rapidly, it grew louder. A fusillade of bullets embedded into the far walls of the room. Then it was quiet. Seconds later, we heard an automobile engine gunning to life, followed rapidly by a second. The squeal of tires ripped the air, and the two cars rapidly moved away.

"Quick," Randy said, "get the book and the document, and give them to me."

I didn't argue or protest. The book, its tooled leather jacket wrapped around the torn-out pages, lay on the sofa where I'd set it after handing the document to Wrenshurst. I picked it up and turned to the professor. The yellowed birth certificate was still clutched in his right hand, which was partially hidden under his lifeless body. I eased the arm out from under him and pried his fingers loose from the brittle paper. Folding it carefully along the original creases, I slipped it between the pages of the book and hurried across to Randy.

Fortunately, the book was not a large one. Randy took it from me and slipped it under his shirt between his back and the top of his slacks. When he dropped his sports jacket back into place, the book was completely hidden.

We heard a car screech to a halt somewhere out in front of the house. Randy eased open the front door. "Officer Randolph McCutcheon," he called out. "Don't fire. I'm coming out."

I could see blue light reflecting on and off against the front door as

Randy pulled it all the way open and stepped through, his hands high above his head, his service revolver dangling between his thumb and forefinger. Moments later, he was surrounded by uniformed police, and a group of them came back through the door. Randy was talking in low, earnest tones to one of them he apparently knew, but I couldn't hear what he was saying.

Everyone made appropriate oohing and aahing sounds at the sight of the dead bodies. I suspected, despite what they said on television or in the movies, that most police officers came into contact with brutally slain corpses far less regularly than we were led to believe.

Before long, two men in suits came through the door—homicide detectives from downtown, who immediately began asking questions. One of the officers was helping two white-uniformed ambulance attendants with the injured man by the front door. I dutifully answered those questions put to me, but beyond that, I volunteered nothing and kept my mouth shut.

I think things were made considerably easier by the fact that Randy was one of the members of the team and had been involved when it had all happened. The fact that I hadn't fired a shot didn't hurt either. I was, in effect and as Randy told it, an innocent bystander.

The living room began to look like an ill-planned and chaotic convention with the arrival of the medical examiner and his assistants, who immediately went to the two dead bodies and knelt down to make their examinations. I thought that if I were to go to the door and look out, the front of the house would look like the forecourt to a used public vehicle lot.

A few moments later, when we left to go down to the Public Safety Building to sign formal statements, my suspicions were proven correct. There was an ambulance just pulling away from the curb, two coroner's wagons, four blue-and-white patrol cars, and the unmarked car the detectives had arrived in. Not to mention my little Datsun.

Randy claimed personal responsibility for me, and the two of us drove downtown together. It was like a parade. Along the way, the blue-and-whites drifted off toward their assigned patrols, and somewhere later we lost the "meat wagons," so by the time we reached our destination, our parade had shortened considerably.

Inside, our statements were taken again by stenographers, who hurried away to have them typed up. We answered a few more questions and helped ourselves to coffee in cardboard cups from the vending machines in the hall. When the stenographers came back with the freshly typed statements, we signed them, duly witnessed by one of the detectives. At no time during any of the proceedings did Randy mention either the book or the birth certificate, which were still secured against his back by his belt.

Randy's service revolver was impounded as evidence, and he was suspended with pay pending an investigation. The Seattle Police had recently been under fire from citizens' groups about unnecessary gunfire from officers trying to do their duty, and no one was taking any chances.

Finally, we were free to go. Randy excused himself for a moment, explaining that he had to get something from his locker. He returned a few minutes later, and we left.

"What did you have to get?" I asked him as we walked to the car.

"This," he said, pushing his jacket open.

I looked down and saw the butt of a small semiautomatic pistol protruding from the waistband of his pants.

12

HY DIDN'T YOU MENTION the book?" I asked him.

We were making our way up Sixth Avenue toward Denny, me driving and Randy slumped back against the passenger seat with his eyes closed.

"I thought it would be better if I didn't," he answered.

"Randy," I pleaded, "we need help. This is bigger than we ever thought. If we don't get some help, I think we're going to be very dead before very long."

His eyes were still closed, and I wasn't sure he'd heard me.

"Randy?"

"I heard you," he said. "I'm thinking."

I drove on, letting him think. At Denny, I turned left and drove west toward the bottom of Queen Anne Hill. Right on First Avenue, north past Seattle Center, then left again on Roy to the foot of the Counterbalance. Still Randy hadn't said a word.

"Well?" I said as the light turned green and I rounded the corner, nosing the car up the hill. "Say something."

He opened his eyes and turned to me. "You're right, Carl. We do need help. But not the local police."

"Why not?"

"Because," he explained to me patiently, "I think this is beyond them.

I think we're dealing with international intrigue here. Foreign agents, possibly. Something that spans history. Hell, I don't know what we're dealing with any more than you do, but I'm sure that whatever it is, it's big. Too big for local police who think in terms of bank robberies and bar brawls and the occasional murder of passion.

"I just don't think they're ready to handle the kind of cold, calculated violence we've seen. And I think we've only seen the tip of what the criminals are capable of."

I thought about that for a few moments. We hit the top of the hill, and I turned left through the four-way stop heading west on our street, then eased the car into the curb across from the apartment building. "So, what do we do?"

"*We* don't do anything," he said. "*I* do it. And what I do is get hold of a friend of mine in Washington who will be able to help."

My head snapped right, and I stared at him. "Washington? DC?"

"That's the one," he said, grinning at me. "Home of the Lincoln Memorial and the Washington Monument."

I suddenly felt very cold. There was more to this man than I had thought. Only I didn't know what it was. Whatever it was, it frightened me. Ordinary city policemen, I reasoned, didn't have close friends sitting in high places in the nation's capital. Not that I'd ever heard, anyway.

"Who are you *really*?" I asked, my voice so low it was barely audible.

He laughed at that. "Why, I'm exactly who you think I am. Just a simple uniformed policeman of a medium-sized city trying his best to help preserve the law and order—and trying to enjoy his private life to the fullest. Which," he added, "has come closer to fullest than it's ever been since I met you. Believe me."

Despite my fears, and despite the foreboding I felt about where we were headed, I blushed. Fortunately, it was dark enough in the car that it went unobserved.

"I don't buy that," I said.

I could have said more, but to what purpose? I'd said enough that he was aware of my disbelief. I just sat there, staring at him, letting it sink in. If we were going to mean anything to each other in a way I could fully accept, our relationship had to be firmly based on trust and truth. Half truths and dark secrets wouldn't suffice.

In the dim light from the streetlamp across from the car, I could see the hard set of his face and the indecision in his eyes as he agonized over what he should say to my accusation. Finally, I assumed, his own similar feelings won out.

"You're right," he said. "There's more to it than that. But I can't explain it to you right now. I just can't, Carl. And I'll have to ask you to trust that. Just a little longer. Will you do that for me? For us?"

My own decision came automatically, from the gut feeling I'd had about Randolph McCutcheon the first time I'd gotten into his patrol car. "I *do* trust you, Randy."

"Thanks," he said, and in that one word he voiced all the relief, all the release from tension I would ever need to hear to know how much he cared about me, how much my trusting him meant to our relationship. "Come on. Let's go in."

We got to the door of the building before I was struck by a terrifying thought. I grabbed his arm, stopping him from going any further. "What if they've been here?" I asked. "You said we'd been followed. So they had to know where we were in order to follow us. Which means they had to know we weren't here."

He took my hand gently in his own and squeezed it tenderly before removing it from his arm. "Believe me," he said, "if anyone got into my apartment while we were gone, then two very large, very capable men will be looking for a new line of employment tomorrow morning."

I stared at him blankly, not comprehending. Or, more correctly, comprehending more than I was capable of assimilating.

He grinned again, disarming my fears. "I'll explain it all in a little while. Come on up, and we'll get a cup of coffee while I make that phone call."

True to his prediction, Randy's apartment hadn't been touched. I didn't know which worried me more: the fact that no one had been able to intrude, which meant whoever was behind the break-ins and the murders—and I was still convinced it was Brunner—would now be doubly resolved in their attempts to recover the document, or the fact that Randy was mixed up with some individual or organization capable of preventing what had already proved to be formidable adversaries from searching his apartment. For the second option implied people who were just as capable and probably just as ruthless as those we were trying to avoid.

I put the coffee on while Randy made his phone call. I could hear him talking in the other room, but his voice was low enough and muffled enough by the distance and the intervening wall to prevent me from understanding what he was saying. A few minutes later, he came into the kitchen and told me he was expecting a return call with instructions about what he should do next.

We were halfway through our second cup of coffee, a strained and somewhat self-conscious silence hanging over the room, when the call came in. Randy took the call in the living room again, so I couldn't hear clearly what was being said.

"I have to go out and meet someone," he told me when he returned. He picked up his cup and drained it. "I shouldn't be too long, and you won't have to worry about anyone coming in while I'm away. As I told you, there are two very large and very capable men outside guarding this place."

He kissed me gently and left. I poured another cup of coffee for myself and lit a cigarette, sitting in the kitchen and reflecting on the mess I'd gotten myself involved in, wondering how it was all going to turn out. I kept hoping it would be somewhat on the positive side, because I'd finally found a reason to go on living that wasn't connected with memories of the past. And suddenly, desperately, I didn't want to lose it.

They had cleaned and bandaged my wound at the police station, but it still throbbed slightly, so I went into Randy's bathroom and rummaged through his medicine cabinet until I found a bottle of aspirin. I took four and then went back to the kitchen and my coffee.

Ten minutes went by, then fifteen, and I was feeling rather depressed and lonely waiting for Randy to come back. As I often do when I'm feeling low, I decided music would help lift my spirits. I crushed out my cigarette and carried my coffee into the living room. The Leonard Pennario recording was still sitting on the turntable, the Rachmaninoff rhapsody facing up. I lifted it off the spindle, turned it over, adjusted the volume, and set the needle down on the record. Seconds later, the jubilant opening strains of Grieg's Concerto in A filled the room. I sat down on the sofa and let the music wash over me, lifting the spirit of depression from my consciousness.

Partway through the slow second movement, I dreamily half opened my eyes, and they fell on the book of *Faust* I'd set on the coffee table when we'd come in. I studied it for a while, deciding it was responsible for all the troubles incurred in the past several days.

Suddenly, I opened my eyes fully and looked at it again. It was sitting there, naked and unprotected, a prime target for the people who wanted it so desperately. It dawned on me that if Brunner got ahold of the book and chose to expose it publicly, it could eventually come to light that my uncle was a Nazi. If the document was traced to my family and the instrumental involvement it had in aiding the Nazi Party, it would no longer make me just Brunner's target but a target of all the groups of people who had been ostracized and persecuted in that era. My reputation and that of my business would forever be tainted by the actions of my uncle and his close connection to Adolf Hitler. This could lead down to my ex-wife and son, whose lives could be incurably endangered by association. The thought of allowing Brunner and his men to put so much I cared about in harm's way—it was overwhelming. But this certificate was the only living proof that Hitler had a twin brother, and it could be used to explain critical gaps in the historical archives. Hence, I couldn't destroy it…but I'd have to hide it somewhere they could never find it. Somewhere out of sight, at least. For, despite Randy's assurances, I had no guarantee that the two men he had posted outside were really capable of fending off half a dozen men or more should they decide to make a concerted effort at breaking in.

After all, I concluded, if they had followed us to Professor Wrenshurst's house, then they would have seen that I had the book—and therefore the document—with me. There would have been no reason for them to search Randy's apartment.

By the same reasoning, they would have seen us return if they were still following us. They would know that I had brought the document back to the apartment. And they would know Randy had left, empty-handed, leaving me here with it, alone.

I bolted off the sofa and snatched the document from between the pages of the book. Two men, no matter how large or capable, wouldn't be able to fend off an army. And for all I knew, that was exactly what we were up against. I had to hide the document. I had to hide it where it wouldn't be found. If Brunner's men found me with the book, they'd probably kill me. But if they found me without the book, they'd have to keep me alive to find where it was hidden.

I walked around the apartment looking for a place to hide it. But remembering the condition of my aunt's home in Bryn Mawr, I began realizing that nowhere in this apartment would really be safe. So what was I to do?

Still holding the yellowed piece of paper, I walked over to the window and looked down at the street. It appeared deserted, although I knew that somewhere down there two men were hidden away in the shadows, keeping watch. And how many others that I didn't know about? How many others just waiting for the perfect opportunity to break in and take the birth certificate away from me?

It wasn't a pleasant thought to contemplate.

I looked up at the sky to study the weather. I could see the moon only partially. It was obscured by the angle of the eaves of the roof and by the thick clouds building up on the horizon. Its light was weak, pale, and scattered, leaving much of the street in deep shadows and illuminating the scene below me with only irregular shafts of pearly, nearly impenetrable luminescence.

Suddenly, glancing up for a second time, I was struck by inspiration. *The roof!* I could hide it on the roof, and they would never find it. They would never think to look there. It was perfect.

If it could be done.

I raced into the bathroom and closed the door behind me, throwing the tiny room into darkness. Of course, if *they* were out there at this very moment and looking at this particular window, then all my efforts would be for nothing. But as I looked out the window, I thought it unlikely.

There were several tall, wide evergreens standing behind the apartment building, effectively blocking that end of the building from view from anywhere but directly below the window. I didn't think they would risk standing that close to the building until they were ready to make their move inside. And if they were that close to effecting a break-in, it was too late to act anyway.

Deciding to work from the assumption that I still had a little time, I opened the window. It was one of those old-fashioned types that opened outward on hinges set in the side of the window, much like a tiny door with glass panes. Holding the window for support, I wriggled through the opening to my waist, twisted around so that I was facing up, and surveyed the roof.

It was built on a rather steep incline and constructed of cedar shingles. In the weak moonlight, I could just make out a scattering of dark patches that were undoubtedly moss—and would undoubtedly be slippery.

Grasping the edge of the roof with my right hand and keeping my left firmly on the top edge of the window, I tried pulling myself upright. I came up off the windowsill easily until I was balanced precariously on the backs of my thighs, one hand on the top of the window, the other curled around the edge of the roof. And at that point, I was stuck. If I let go with either hand in order to gain new purchase, my own weight would carry me backward. And I had no desire to drop five stories to the ground below.

I was just concluding that getting up on the roof was either impossible or would require some additional equipment when my right hand slipped. My stomach rushed upward into the back of my throat as I felt that familiar and terrifying sensation of falling. My knees hooked over the windowsill as I went backward, and I could feel my left hand losing its grip on the window.

With the desperation born of the will to survive, I arched my right arm over my head and brought my right hand down on the top of the window. My hand, moving too fast, smashed into the window with a painful jar that sent further twinges of pain shooting up my arm, causing my bullet wound to throb severely. The force with which my hand hit the window came so unexpectedly that it startled me into letting go with my left hand. The left side of my body dropped away, leaving me dangling by my knees and my severely pained right hand.

I could feel the pain in my hand turning to numbness, and my fingers began to slide over the slick, worn wood of the window frame. A few more seconds, and I would be dropping over backward with only my knees holding me from falling to a sure death five stories below. The windowsill itself was too wide for my knees to grip it effectively, and I knew with certainty that if my hand slipped, I would fall within moments.

Frantically, I twisted my body upward, using all the strength I could find to bring my left arm up toward the window. I was too far out of shape for this kind of gymnastic endeavor, and it showed. The fingers of my left hand grazed the bottom of the window, and I dropped backward again. The downward jolt caused the fingers of my right hand to slip even farther toward the point where they would be holding nothing but air.

My desperation turned to terror. Mustering all the strength I could find, I thrust my left arm upward once again. This time, the tips of my fingers and thumb curled around the edge of the window frame, giving me a precarious hold. I wriggled my fingers inward until I had a firm grasp on the window and then eased my weight from my right arm to my left. With the weight off my strained, tiring right arm, it was fairly easy to slide my right hand up and over the top of the window.

I transferred my weight back again despite the protests of the aching muscles in my right arm, and in a series of crablike motions, I moved my left hand up the window until it hooked over the top. With both hands on top of the window, and using the window for support, I wriggled my body back through the window until my feet touched the floor. Two seconds later I was back in the bathroom, down on my knees being violently sick. I had never come so close to dying in my life. It was not something I cared to experience again.

Yet I would have to face it again if I was to hide the birth certificate on the roof. And I'd already determined, short of leaving the building, that the roof was the safest, least-likely-to-be-searched place to hide it.

I went back into the living room and lit a cigarette to calm my nerves. Dragging the smoke into my lungs greedily, I sat down on the couch and gradually began to breathe in a normal rhythm. The taste in my mouth from being sick was more than a little unpleasant, so when I'd finished the cigarette, I went into the kitchen, found a half-empty bottle of Scotch in the cupboard, and downed two quick swallows right from the bottle.

It burned and clawed its way down my throat and left me feeling much steadier.

I'd tucked the document inside my shirt before crawling out the window, and fortunately my inept aerial exhibition hadn't dislodged it. I wasn't sure I'd be so lucky on my next attempt, so I decided to take some precautions. Glancing down at my watch, I saw only ten minutes had elapsed since I'd first walked into the bathroom to examine the feasibility of climbing onto the roof. Maybe my time had already run out. They could barge through the door at any moment. But I pushed the thought aside and carried on with my preparations as if I had all the time in the world.

Remembering the clouds gathering on the horizon, I realized the document would have to be kept safe from water damage. A good soaking in the rain could dissolve it into worthless, unreadable pulp. Searching through the drawers in Randy's kitchen, I found exactly what I needed.

First, I wrapped the folded document in two layers of waxed paper. Then I sealed all the open edges with plastic tape. This package I inserted into one of those ziplock plastic sandwich bags. Then, as an extra precaution, I slipped the bag into a larger ziplock bag.

Satisfied that the paper was safe from water damage, I set about figuring out a way to get it up on the roof. My first intention had been to crawl far enough onto the roof that it would be totally out of sight to anyone who might take a notion to poke his head out the window and peer up. After my near fall, I revised my plan to placing the package just up over the lip of the roof in such a way that my body would have to travel the least possible distance out the window.

Now, after taking the time to wrap the document in waterproofing, I'd had time to reassess my plan. As much as I disliked my conclusion, I decided that the farther up the roof, the better. The people I was dealing with were clever as well as resourceful. If they didn't find it in the apartment, and if they could determine that I hadn't left the apartment to hide it elsewhere in the building, then the windows would be the only logical choice left. I didn't doubt for a minute they'd at least poke their heads out and take a look. So it was up on the roof for me.

I took a wide piece of plastic tape and secured the plastic-wrapped document to my chest beneath my shirt, Then, rummaging in the drawers, I found a knife with a short, thick blade and a handle long enough for me to grasp. I also found a sturdy screwdriver. In another drawer, I found a slim hammer and a box of long-pointed nails. With my loot in hand, I went back to the bathroom.

I slipped the box of nails into my front pocket and pushed the hammer through my belt at the back of my pants so it would be out of my way. I closed the door behind me, so the room was dark except for the faint illumination from the moon. The odor of my stomach's upheaval still lingered, reminding me of my near demise on my first attempt. I ignored it. I opened the window, crawled through, and twisted over so I was facing up.

Using the knife first, I brought my right arm down with as much force as I could, embedding the short, sturdy blade into the cedar shingles. It sank clean up to the haft. I pulled and tugged against it with all my strength, but it held. Satisfied as I would ever be that it would hold my weight, I pulled myself up so my feet were on the windowsill and rammed the screwdriver into the roof farther up. It also held, and I blessed the building's owner for having gone so long without reroofing. Years of weathering had rendered the normally hard cedar a soft, mushy texture.

Alternating the knife and the screwdriver, I pulled myself farther and farther up the roof until I found myself at the base of the brick chimney that served as an exhaust vent for the furnace in the basement. An indentation had been cut into the roof to accommodate the chimney, leaving a flat horizontal surface about eight inches in width around the base of the brick structure. Cautiously holding on to the embedded screwdriver, I reached into my shirt and peeled off the tape that had secured the plastic-wrapped parcel to my skin. Not having anticipated the ramifications of sticking tape against my chest, I suffered silently in brief, scorching pain. At any rate, the parcel fit perfectly on the level section. What was more, the chimney on one side and the vertical slope of the indentation on the other three sides provided a natural barrier from the wind, making it virtually impossible for a storm to blow the package away.

I pulled the box of nails from my pocket and scattered a number of them on the ledge. Then, easing the hammer from my belt and using only my free right hand, I proceeded to pound nails into the edges of the large ziplock bag. It was a tedious process trying to force the nails in with my hand far enough to stand upright so that I could then pound them in with the hammer, but I didn't dare let go my hold on the screwdriver for fear of sliding backward and off the roof. Eventually, though, I had enough nails in to satisfy myself that there was no chance that a gust would lift the parcel off the roof.

I left the hammer where it was, next to the half-empty box of nails, and started the journey back down the roof, again alternating between the knife and the screwdriver. There was one uncomfortable moment when one of the shingles shattered and the knife blade came loose, but I still had most of my weight on the implanted screwdriver at that point. I restruck with the knife and continued down.

A few minutes later, I was safely back inside the bathroom, vowing that when the time came to retrieve the birth certificate, Randy would be the one to go up and fetch it. As far as I was concerned, I had climbed the roof for the last time.

I poured myself another cup of coffee and settled down to await whoever might come through the apartment door. At that point, I wasn't sure who would make it first.

13

RANDY WAS THE FIRST to arrive, by minutes.

He came in breathing hard, his face flushed. He must have skipped the elevator and run up all five flights of stairs.

I'd heard the key in the lock, and for a moment I'd held my breath, not sure who it was—hoping it would be Randy but not convinced his two burly goons downstairs were really up to repelling boarders. When he came through the door huffing and puffing, I breathed a long sigh of relief.

"You look relieved," he said between gasps for air.

"I wasn't sure it would be you. You were gone longer than I thought you'd be."

He tried for a grin and succeeded in giving me a half contortion with the right side of his mouth. "Yeah, well, it took longer to get to the airport than I thought it would."

"The airport? You couldn't have driven all the way down to Sea-Tac and back."

"Not Sea-Tac," he explained, still puffing. "Boeing Field. Private jet."

"Oh, I see," I said, not seeing at all. "Well, tell me, what did you find there?"

"The man waiting downstairs in your car," he said.

I hadn't even realized he'd taken it, and I was just about to say something to the effect that next time he could jolly well ask if he could take the car when he interrupted me.

"I've got to take the birth certificate down to him. Then we're going to move him and the document to a safe house while he examines it. Where is it? I don't have much time."

I held my hand up in the universal symbol for stop, palm forward. "Hold on there a minute, old buddy. The document is safely tucked away for the moment. And it's going to stay there until you tell me what's going on."

"Carl, please," he said, almost begging, "there isn't time for this right now."

I shook my head. "You'd better make time for it, Randy, because that document is staying right where it is until I get some answers." I had risked my life hiding the document to protect it. I couldn't bear the thought of the tremendous trouble I'd gone to being all for naught.

His eyes pleaded with me. "Carl, is this really necessary? Couldn't it wait for a little while? I thought you said you trusted me."

That last was a low blow, especially considering I had so recently been thinking that any future relationship we might build had to be based on trust. And I *wanted* to trust him. I really did.

But I also wanted to know just what the heck was going on.

"I *do* trust you, Randy. Believe me. But sometimes trust isn't enough. Sometimes facts are required. And this is one of those times."

I deliberately took my time sitting down on the sofa and lighting a cigarette with a flourish of my lighter while he stood there, mute, looking helpless.

"Now then," I said, "I have been chased by God knows who in an automobile up the freeway, my house has been destroyed by vandals that still have to be apprehended, I have been threatened in my own office by a man waving a gun in my face, I have been placed under surveillance and followed, I have been shot at by persons unknown while watching an old friend get his head blown off. I have had my life threatened over the telephone." I took a deep breath. "And, if that weren't enough, the man I think I'm in love with has as much as admitted to me that he isn't who he claims to be but is really in league with some mysterious organization in Washington that he *says* he can't talk to me about."

He gave me a peculiar look, and then said, "Say that again?"

I breathed a long sigh of annoyance. "I said, I was chased—"

"Not that part. The part at the end."

"Oh, Randy, really!" I snapped. "I said that you as much as admitted to me that you belonged—"

Again, he cut me off. "No, the part about the man you think you're in love with."

He stood there, his eyes shining, defenseless. It was more than I could take. "I said that you're the man I think I'm in love with. That's crazy, isn't it? I mean, I barely know you. Love doesn't happen that fast, does it? I mean, I don't think it does."

"Sometimes it does," he said, his words so low I almost didn't hear them. "I think it happened to me."

I sat there, staring at him. I didn't know for how long. The cigarette burned unnoticed between my fingers. Finally, the heat of it penetrated my consciousness, and I stubbed it out in the ashtray in front of me.

"You're serious, aren't you?"

He nodded his head once. "Yes."

I was up off the sofa before I realized what I was doing, taking him in my arms and kissing him. He kissed me back, and there was no mistaking the genuineness of his passion.

"Oh, God, Randy," I croaked, "I hoped, but I didn't think it could be possible."

"I know," he murmured in my ear. "I know."

We kissed again, then he gently pried me away from him. "There really isn't much time," he said. "What do you want to know?"

"Who do you work for? Really?" I asked him.

"I work for a group called the Committee," he told me. And then he quickly explained, leaving out nothing important but skipping the irrelevant details.

The Committee, it seemed, had been formed by a tiny core group within the various intelligence services working out of the federal government. These six men had gotten together through the conviction that their own services were too tied up in government red tape in some circumstances, possibly infiltrated by agents of foreign powers in others, and becoming lax in their efforts at handling difficult assignments in still others.

These six men had therefore decided to fund and train a small, elite group of agents drawn completely from outside their own agencies. Each of these agents would know only the man who had made the initial contact, the name of the organization, and the reason for its existence.

"All the agents," he explained, "are carefully screened under a variety of pretexts. None of them knows who any of the others are, nor how many there are. All the agents, as I understand it, go about their regular jobs except in those situations that the Committee deems it necessary to pull them off to assign them."

"You really are a cop, then?"

"Yes, I really am," he said. "I was contacted while I was still in the academy. I listened to the pitch, I thought it made sense, and, after thinking it over for a few weeks, I met my contact again and said yes. It was that simple."

"None of it sounds simple to me," I argued. "You said you were carefully screened. I take it they missed the fact you were gay?"

"No, not at all," he said. "In fact, they decided that fact alone made me perfect for the job they had in mind for me right from the beginning."

"And just what might that have been?" I asked, suddenly growing suspicious.

"Why," he said, as if he were stating the obvious, "keeping watch over you. And I must admit that until that guy got into your office the other night and you called the police, I haven't done a very good job of it."

I was very confused. "Why would they have wanted someone keeping watch over me? It doesn't make sense."

I could see he was growing impatient again. He glanced down at his watch. "It made sense in their shoes, apparently. I just found this out coming back from the airport. It seems the existence of this document has been theorized for quite some time."

"It's been a well-kept secret, then," I said bitterly.

"Yes, it has," he said. "Like I said, I just found out about it myself. You remember what the professor said. Some experts thought it wasn't Hitler who died in the bunker but a double of some sort. The only thing that made that unlikely was the thorough examination of the corpse. There was no evidence of plastic surgery. There was no evidence of any kind to suggest that the man who died wasn't exactly who he should have been.

"But here and there over the years, there have been persistent rumblings that Adolf Hitler is still alive and directing the new rise in the Nazi Party that has been occurring over the last eight or ten years. Most experts dismiss those rumors as just that—rumors to stir the hearts of the faithful.

"However, one man sat down and made a logical analysis of the situation, concluding that if there was an unknown twin and the twin was substituted toward the end of the war, Hitler would have been able to escape Germany undetected to carry on his avowed mission in secret. Apparently, no one took him seriously until one of the members of the Committee chanced upon the story."

"So this whole time you've been deceiving me? Playing along with me and acting astounded when I had the idea of looking inside the binding?"

"Carl, I couldn't be sure, and I wanted to keep my assignment clandestine for as long as possible. If I'd been more assertive, I would have blown my cover and possibly lost your trust in the process."

That made enough sense.

He looked at his watch again, pointedly. "There isn't any more time, Carl. Where's the document? We've got to get it to a safe place."

"I'll get it for you," I said. "But one more question first. Why did they think *I* should be watched? I mean, why me? Why did they think the document would end up with me?"

"A lot of that is still unclear to me," he confessed. "But I did ask. It seems you weren't the only one who was being watched. There were four others."

"But how did they know to watch us in the first place?"

"I'm not sure. I told you—the men in the Committee are men in very high positions. Men with access to a great deal of classified material. Men who could gain entrance to the archives of material captured at the end of the war. Material, as I understand it, that has never come close to being inventoried and catalogued. But much of it has. So when they began to investigate the possibility that the Hitler twin theory might be true, they started going through old documents, old personnel records, things like that.

"Eventually, somehow—and don't ask me how—they narrowed down the list of possibilities of those men close to Hitler at the end of the war who might have been able to smuggle the document out of the country. If, indeed, that document existed.

"In your case, it was your uncle Rolf. If it was him, then, you became the next possibility for possessing it, with both him and his wife dead. You, after all, were in line to inherit. As I understand it, they never seriously considered that you knew anything about it. Only that if it existed, and if your uncle was the one who carried it out of Germany, it might somehow end up in your hands.

"It was my job to watch you and see if anyone tried to make some kind of contact with you about it. For, they reasoned, if the document existed, then whoever would need to possess it would know exactly where it had been all these years. And, apparently, the waiting time is over."

"The waiting time for what?" I asked.

But he never had time to answer. At that moment, the door to the apartment burst open, slamming back into the wall with a loud crash.

Randy whirled around, his hand grabbing at the revolver in his belt. But he never stood a chance. The first of the two men through the door already had his pistol drawn. He fired it once, and I watched Randy fall backward, striking his head against the corner of the coffee table before he landed in a heap on the floor. I think I screamed, but I'm not sure.

The first man stepped aside, and the second man stepped into the room. I could see at least two more out in the hall, and I didn't even have to guess what had happened to the two burly, so-called capable men who had been guarding the outside of the building. Without being told, I knew they would never be guarding anything else again.

The second man through the door was also holding a gun. I had seen that type of handgun before, only always on the silver screen in Second World War movies. It was a huge, black, ugly German Luger.

I had also seen the man who held it before. He addressed me in his curious, flat voice. "We meet again, Mr. Traeger."

"So it would appear," I said. My eyes wanted to look down at Randy, but I couldn't take them off my visitor.

Again, the curious, flat voice: "You have something I want."

What could I say to that?

14

WHAT I DID SAY was "You can go to hell!"

I could tell he wasn't used to being treated like that. Especially not in front of his subordinates. His mouth twisted into a mute snarl of anger as he took two quick strides toward me. Then, without warning, his right arm came up across his body and slashed downward in a savage blow. The end of the barrel of his Luger caught me high on the cheekbone, tearing a gash down the side of my face almost to the corner of my mouth.

The blow caught me completely off guard, sending me reeling back. I fell heavily on my left side, most of my weight landing with bone-jarring impact on my left elbow and forearm. My whole left arm went numb.

Where I'd fallen wasn't very far from Randy's prone figure. I glanced over at him and felt overwhelmed by grief and remorse at what I'd led him into. And the way it had turned out for him. The position in which he lay was obscuring the severity of his wound, but I caught sight of blood dripping against his neck. Before I had a chance to look away, he flicked his eyes open. I saw his chest rise and fall slightly as he took a shallow breath. He was still alive!

I was about to say so, to insist on Luger-Fist getting him some help. My shock must have registered on my face, because before I could speak, Randy stopped me with an almost imperceptible negative movement of his head. If I hadn't been staring at him directly, as close as I was, I never would have seen it.

Turning quickly to look up at the man with the gun, I began to groan. I sat upright and massaged my left arm, trying to bring some feeling back into it. It wasn't all an act; my arm was both numb and hurting like hell at the same time. Slowly, still rubbing my arm, I stood up. "That make you feel better?" I asked him sullenly. My fingers went to my face and came away smeared with blood.

He didn't waste any time apologizing. "As I said, Mr. Traeger, you have something that belongs to me. I think it would be better all around if you simply let me have it."

There was no anger in his voice—just quiet, confident menace. The kind that promised I would suffer exquisitely if I didn't turn the document over to him. And rather quickly, at that.

But, I thought suddenly, what guarantee was there that I wouldn't suffer anyway once I'd given him the paper? And as quickly as I thought it, the answer came: none whatsoever. They couldn't let me live, certainly, after they'd let me see them shoot Randy down in cold blood. I could identify them. Easily, and with pleasure. And if all I'd seen and read was true, the police would become ruthless and more than efficiently effective when tracking down someone who had murdered one of their own. I figured these men must be at least as familiar with that fact as I was.

An idea came to me then. One I thought might confuse them sufficiently to force them to contact their superiors for new instructions. And I didn't doubt for a moment that they had superiors. Luger-Fist was tough, all right, but he didn't look particularly bright. And I already knew he wasn't Brunner. I was positive that Brunner was running this show.

"I'm afraid I can't help you," I said.

He took a step forward, raising the Luger for another swing. Feigning fright as best I could—which wasn't all that difficult—I backed away from him, my hands held awkwardly in front of my face for protection. "It's not that I don't want to help you," I said hurriedly. "Not that I wouldn't if I could. It's that I *can't* help you. I don't have it any longer!"

He lowered the Luger, his placid look replaced by confusion. "What do you mean you don't have it?"

In backing away from him, I'd taken great care to move away from where Randy lay on the floor, apparently dead. I didn't want them too close to him. I glanced down at him and pointed abruptly. Just as abruptly, I snapped my head back to look at Luger-Fist, forcing him to look away from Randy in order to watch my face.

"What I mean is I gave him the paper after that little debacle at Professor Wrenshurst's house. He took it away this afternoon, and he didn't bring it back." I forced myself to include a slight catch in my voice, as if I were in immediate danger of breaking into tears. "And now you've gone and killed him!"

Luger-Fist's confusion deepened as he looked back at Randy and then again at me. "You're lying."

I hung my head and wiped nonexistent tears from my eyes. "I wish I were," I said melodramatically. "It would save us both a lot of trouble."

Luger-Fist looked back down at Randy's body, and for a moment I thought he was going to check more closely, on the chance that he wasn't really dead. If I was telling him the truth, Randy was the only one who knew where the document was. And if Randy was still alive, I had no doubts that Luger-Fist would inflict all the pain necessary to force him to reveal its location.

The problem was that Randy didn't know where I'd hidden it. I simply couldn't allow them to examine him. I knew I wasn't strong enough to stand by and watch him be tortured for information he didn't possess just to save myself. And what would that gain us anyway?

The answer to that, I knew, was nothing. They would end up killing

Randy anyway once they realized he didn't possess the information they wanted. Then they'd start in on me.

"Before you smashed your way in here," I said, in the best accusatory tone I could manage, while turning my back on him and taking another several steps away from Randy, "he told me he'd taken the document somewhere to have it authenticated." I whirled to face him, knowing my abrupt movement would force him to look from Randy's fallen body to me. "I don't know where he took it, but he did tell me he actually worked for some agency out of Washington. Some supersecret group. He didn't tell me which one, but I'm sure you have the resources to find out."

Then, not being able to resist the dig, I added, "Or your superiors do, at any rate."

My reminder that he was not the man in charge, not even of his own life, but that he obeyed orders from someone higher up, hit him where I'd hoped it would—his pride. He drew himself up to his full height, holding himself stiffly. His eyes narrowed, going cold and menacing. With his left hand, he signaled to the two men who, I could see, were still standing outside the door as he snapped off short commands in German. The two men came through the door on the run, and each grabbed me by an arm.

I put up some token resistance and then allowed them to drag me toward the door, resisting the impulse to look back at Randy. As we went, I couldn't help but wonder if I'd ever see him again.

The elevator was at the far end of the hall, but Luger-Fist and his cohorts judiciously avoided it, opting instead for the stairs that ran down the rear wall of the building. We'd just rounded the landing between the first and second floors when I spotted a middle-aged woman with a basket of laundry maneuvering herself through the steel fire door between the stairwell and the first-floor hallway. Instinctively, I knew I would never have another chance like the one she had unwittingly presented to me.

"Help!" I shouted. "Call the police! I'm being kidnapped!"

I suppose if I'd taken time to think about it, I never would have chanced it. I certainly had no desire to see an innocent woman suffer, and later, when I analyzed what I'd done, I could very clearly see that she might have been brutally maimed or even killed. But I didn't think about it—I just did it.

The woman looked up the stairwell at us, shock and fear springing to her face. "Help!" I screamed again.

She appeared to move in slow motion as she dropped her laundry basket and jumped through the door. Fortunately for her, the basket was able to push the door shut behind her. I could almost see her running to her apartment to telephone the police. But I didn't have time to dwell on it.

As I'd hoped, my unexpected cries for help brought on reflexive self-protective movements from the two men who were holding my arms. Without pause, both of them let me go and reached for the weapons concealed in their belts. Luger-Fist had prudently tucked his own weapon out of sight against the probability that some curious onlooker might see it and raise embarrassing questions. He was standing behind me—ready, no doubt, to draw the Luger and use it if I tried to accomplish anything as stupid as a getaway. So, for that split second, no one had a weapon trained on me.

I took one step forward down the stairs while reaching across my body toward the man on my left. Grabbing his right coat sleeve with both hands, I yanked him sideways. He was already slightly off balance as he attempted to reach for his gun, and he toppled easily, crashing into the man on my right. As I leaped down the stairs to the first-floor landing, I could see the two of them going down like bowling pins, their arms flailing over their heads as they tried to break their fall. Behind them, Luger-Fist's long, deadly pistol was just clearing his belt.

Grabbing the knob atop the railing post at the foot of the stairs, I swung myself around in a 180-degree arc and bolted down the steps to the midfloor landing between the first floor and the basement. The back door to the building led from that landing to the parking lot behind. I crashed into the handle that ran the width of the door, allowing my body weight and momentum to depress it, and then I was through and into the chill, damp air outside. I heard a gunshot behind me as I went through the door, and then another. I could also hear Luger-Fist screaming at his two henchmen to get out of his way.

I didn't have the keys to my car; they were still upstairs in Randy's pocket. And I knew I didn't have time to jump the ignition wires—even if I'd known how. Even if I'd been lucky and Randy had left the car unlocked. So I raced across the parking lot and plunged through a narrow opening in the hedge that separated it from the apartment building on the other side of the block. I glanced behind me and saw Luger-Fist coming through the door, his right arm extended out in front of him. I didn't have to see the Luger to know it was there.

I ducked sideways and fell flat against the ground as the gunshot sounded. In front of where I'd been standing, I saw the ground kick up a shower of dirt clods, silhouetted by the dim light over the rear door of the building in front of me.

That light also revealed a narrow walkway running along the side of the building, presumably leading to the street beyond. Half running and half crawling, trying to stay down below any more gunshots that might be aimed in my direction, I made it to the walkway and disappeared into the shadows along the side of the building. Seconds later, I was on the street.

I knew Luger-Fist and his fellows couldn't be far behind me, and I felt particularly vulnerable standing there on the street, unarmed, with the light from the streetlamps illuminating me neatly for anyone who cared to look. I figured they'd be on me before I had a chance to raise an alarm. Nor did I figure I could get back across the block farther down and hope to catch a bus before they caught up with me. Chances were they'd left someone behind just to cover that possibility.

I darted across the street even as I was assessing the situation, angling my path away from the walk where I'd emerged onto the street. Three houses down, I ducked into a drive and faded into the darkness behind an old two-story house. Stopping to catch my breath, I peered around the corner of the building just in time to see Luger-Fist and two of his men step from the shadows of the walk into the light from the streetlamp I'd just been under. They were looking uncertainly up and down the street.

I jerked my head back and moved silently toward the rear of the building. Fortunately, there didn't seem to be any dogs about to raise the alarm.

I didn't think they'd chance going back into Randy's apartment building with the arrival of the police almost certainly imminent. If the woman with the laundry had actually called the police. Remembering the look of fear on her face, I felt sure that she had. However, I didn't think it such a good idea for me to try to return there either.

So what *was* I to do?

There was nothing I could do but keep going, away from Luger-Fist and his pals, trying to put as much distance between us as I could while hoping something brilliant would occur to me.

For half an hour, I made my way through people's yards and apartment building parking lots. All the time I moved, I was aware my journey was taking me downhill. I'd never been in this particular neighborhood before, but I was certain that eventually, moving in the direction I was heading, I would reach Elliott Avenue. It was the main artery into the city from Ballard to the northwest, and as such, it was heavily traveled. Hopefully, once I reached it, I'd be able to find some help. One way or another.

Another half hour brought me pretty much where I'd expected to be. My left pant leg was torn where I'd caught it on a nail in a picket fence I'd been forced to climb over. The right side of my face felt swollen, throbbing painfully from the blow Luger-Fist had administered. But earlier, I'd determined the bleeding had stopped. I was exhausted and out of breath from constant running between shadowed areas. Once, I had surprised a sleeping dog in someone's backyard, forcing me to retreat unceremoniously. The dog, thankfully, had been chained and unable to follow. But he'd raised such a racket that I stood for five minutes behind a huge tree of some kind, peering in the direction I'd just come from. No one emerged from the shadows, and eventually the dog stopped barking.

Heading down Elliott toward the city proper, I came to a telephone booth tucked back against an old wooden storefront. My hand fished a handful of change from my pocket. I left the phone booth door open, not wanting to risk exposure from the overhead light that would come on when the door was pulled closed. I deposited the required number of coins and dialed the only person I knew who might help me out of this situation without asking too many questions: Judy Grenoble.

My watch read about twenty minutes past midnight. I hoped she was home and not engaged in something that might prove embarrassing if I asked her to disentangle herself. She answered on the fifth ring, and I could tell by the sound of her voice when she said hello that I had woken her.

"Judy, this is Carl." Then, with no preliminaries, I said, "I'm in trouble, and I need your help. It's urgent."

She came out of her sleep almost immediately. "Carl?"

I told her again that I needed her help.

"Where are you?" she asked.

I told her. "Can you come and pick me up?"

"What is it, Carl?" She sounded anxious and worried. I was sure she hadn't gotten too many frantic pleas before for help in the middle of the night.

"I don't have time to explain it now," I told her. "Will you trust me?"

"Of course. You know that." No hesitation. She was some girl, all right. "I'll be there in twenty minutes."

"When you get here," I instructed her, "pull into the curb and turn your lights off so only your parking lights are on. Then turn your headlights back on. Then back off to only your parking lights again. You have that?"

She repeated it back to me.

"Good girl," I said. "I'll be waiting for you."

Before I could hang up, she said, "Carl, a package was hand delivered to you at the store this evening. Right before closing. I don't know what it is, or how important. I was going to call you, but I couldn't get Randy's number. It's unlisted."

"Is it still at the store?" I asked, feeling a vague sense of alarm. For all I knew, it could be a bomb of some sort.

"No. I didn't want to leave it, so I brought it home with me."

If it was a bomb, I concluded swiftly, then it most likely would have gone off by now. Still, there was no sense in not taking precautions. Trying to keep any concern or urgency out of my voice, I said, "Listen, Judy. It's probably nothing. But it *could* be a bomb. I don't think it is, but it could be. I want you to carefully wrap the package in as many blankets as you can find. Then carry it downstairs into the basement and leave it in the middle of the laundry room. Will you do that for me?"

She said she would. With the added delay, she revised her arrival time to thirty minutes. I thanked her again and hung up.

There wasn't a lot of traffic on Elliott at that time of night, but there was enough to keep me back in the shadows of the building. The wait seemed to go on forever, but it was actually only twenty-three minutes. Judy's car pulled up in front of the building, and I watched her lights flick through the prearranged sequence. Satisfied that it was her, I slipped out of the shadows and joined her. She moved the car quickly away from the curb and headed back toward her apartment.

As she drove, I filled her in on what had happened, omitting only the details of where I'd hidden the document. I could see the shock and disbelief on her face in the dim light of the car's instrument panel, but I knew she believed every word I told her. She could see the dried, bloody gash on my face for herself.

"You're sure Randy's all right?" she asked.

"Pretty sure," I answered, feeling my stomach knot up at the thought that I'd unwittingly left him there to bleed to death.

"Just out of curiosity, where did you store the document?"

"I think it's better if you don't know, Judy."

A look of disappointment grew on her face. Perhaps she felt dismayed that I didn't trust her enough. But I didn't want to put her in any danger, and if she didn't know where I'd hidden it, she'd be safer.

She parked her car in front of her apartment building on the west side of Capitol Hill, and we slipped around to the rear door. Using her key, she let us in.

"I think I'd better go downstairs and see about that package," I said.

"I'm coming with you."

I looked back at her. "I think it would be safer if you stayed here."

Her face set itself into a mask of firm fury. "I'm coming with you, Carl Traeger, and that's that."

I didn't want to take the time to argue with her—not that it would have done any good. And I'd already decided it probably wasn't a bomb in the package, so I said, "Suit yourself."

We went down the steps into the basement and turned the corner. Ahead of me, I could see the yellow square of light coming through the laundry room door. I stopped. I'd suggested the laundry room because, if it was like other apartment buildings I'd been in, the floor and walls would be composed of concrete. Strong enough, I hoped, to help contain whatever blast might occur. The other reason was my belief that no one would be down in the basement doing their laundry at half past midnight.

Turning to Judy, I asked, "Did you leave the light on?"

She nodded.

"OK, then. Let's go."

A large, haphazard bundle of blankets and towels lay heaped in the center of the floor. From the looks of it, she'd wrapped the package in every strip of cloth she could ransack from her apartment. Motioning her to stay where she was, I went to the bundle and began removing the blankets.

The package was about a foot and a half long by a foot wide and a foot deep. It was wrapped in brown paper, taped with cellophane. No strings or rope. Gently, I ripped the paper off it. The box inside was ordinary, cheap cardboard.

I glanced once at Judy, who stood apprehensively by the door. Then I pulled open the box. Inside was a large bag of thick green plastic. A throwaway garbage bag, I realized. It had a sturdy twist tie around the top.

I lifted the bag from the box, carried it over beneath the single overhead light, and opened it. What I saw inside made me gag. It was a cat—or, rather, what was left of a cat that had been brutally hacked to pieces. But even in that quick glance, there was enough of it left to convince me it had been Paul's cat, Oliver.

I set the bag gently on the floor, walked to the corner of the room, and sagged down to my knees. Then I was quietly and unceremoniously sick.

15

UPSTAIRS, JUDY HAD LET me use her bathroom to clean myself up. Now I was sitting on her davenport with a large glass of neat whiskey in my hand, trying to calm down. The whiskey was Scotch, and the brand had been Paul's favorite. Judy had caught me looking at it as she poured it for me, and, knowing full well that I knew she never drank anything stronger than an occasional sloe gin fizz, she'd remarked that she kept it around the apartment just in case.

She waited until I'd had two good swallows of the Scotch, then crossed over to me and handed me a piece of paper folded into quarters. "I saw this in the bottom of the box while you were being—" She stopped. "While you were in the corner."

I took it from her and opened it. It contained a message, neatly typed: "This could as easily have been a loved one. Brunner." That was all it said. But it was enough to get the message across. Hand over the document, or someone is going to suffer. Someone I cared about.

Someone like Randy, maybe. Or Judy.

I couldn't think of anyone else they could use as leverage against me.

I gulped down the rest of the whiskey and set the glass down. Judy brought the bottle and asked if I wanted another. I shook my head.

Judy had been there for me when there was no one else to care for my existence. Shortly after Paul brought her into the fold at the bookstore,

Judy became more like family to us than just an employee. And she'd proven that to be true when I'd needed her the most. However, we got even closer after Paul left us. I isolated myself from the rest of the world and shut everyone out. That was when Judy struck me, becoming instrumental in forcing me to socialize again. She prevented me from letting my self-inflicted seclusion detrimentally carry me away. If she hadn't exerted so much energy befriending me, I don't know where I'd be now. I had an unhealthy tendency of disengaging myself from others, just as I had detached myself from Margaret and Eric all those years ago. But Judy showed up right on time for me to break that poor habit and start living again. It was at times like these that I realized how fortunate I was to have her in my life. She was always in my corner, with the best of intentions.

"Judy, I've been thinking. I don't think I should stay here. It won't take them too long to figure out this is a place I might go to hide."

She sat down beside me. "I don't think you should leave."

I looked at her curiously. "You don't want these hooligans breaking in on you and tearing your place apart, possibly hurting you in the process, do you?"

"Of course not," she said quietly. "But if they do come, how will they know you're not here unless they break in to find out? And if you *are* gone, I'll be left here to fight them off by myself. You don't want *that*, do you?"

I could see her point. Once again, I had involved an innocent party in what was happening to me. But just as clearly as I saw that I couldn't leave her there on her own, I saw she would have become involved whether I'd called her or not—simply because I knew her and we were close. Brunner would use every bit of leverage against me that he could find.

As he'd used the cat.

"Right," I said. "The only solution, then, is to pack up and get out of here until this is cleared up. Someplace where they can't possibly find you. You don't happen to know anyplace like that, do you?"

It took her only a moment to come up with an answer. "I have a sister down in Portland. I could go down there and stay with her for a while. But I don't want to. What about the bookstore?"

"You let me worry about the bookstore," I said. "The worst that could happen is that it goes out of business. Better the store than you or me."

She gave me one of her concerned, anxious looks, but before she could argue the point, I added, "I don't think we're going to go out of business. I've got enough money to see us through any temporary slump that might occur. And tomorrow morning I'll call the clerks to give them some explanation. Then I'll ask them to look after the place for a few days. One way or another, I'm going to see this wound up by then. OK?"

She hesitated, and I could see she clearly didn't like it, but she finally said she'd do what I asked.

"All right, then," I said. "You go back to sleep. I don't want you driving all the way down to Portland tired. I'll stand guard, and I'll wake you up at about six."

She gave me an impulsive kiss on the cheek and disappeared into the bedroom, leaving the door open. I poured another drink and settled down in a chair near the door. I had no idea what I'd do if any of Brunner's men showed up, but I was too much on edge to sleep. And I knew Judy would sleep better knowing I was out there.

As the hours ticked away, I had plenty of time to think about Randy and wonder if he was all right. I was tempted several times to call the police and inquire, but I didn't know what I would say. Ordinary, innocent citizens didn't normally call up the police and inquire into the health of specific officers. Chances were they wouldn't tell me anything even if I did call. Or so I reasoned.

I had noticed the telephone number printed on the little sticker on Randy's telephone, and telephone numbers were something I rarely forgot. It was a strange mental quirk of mine that I'd never really been able to analyze. Give me zip codes or addresses, and five minutes later I'd have forgotten them completely. But not phone numbers. Seeing a phone number once always seemed to etch it permanently in my brain.

At about four in the morning, I picked up the phone and dialed Randy's number on the off chance he was sitting there waiting for my call. I was just about to hang up when someone picked up the receiver on the other end, and a voice I'd never heard before said hello and then asked me who I was. I slammed the receiver down so hard that I thought surely Judy would wake up from the noise. But she slept through it like a baby.

And, like a baby, I shook with terror. All I could figure was that I'd been wrong. They had gone back to the apartment anticipating that I would return. I shook for almost twenty minutes before the terror subsided. Then I rewarded myself with another stiff slug of the Scotch, vowing it would be my last. I couldn't afford to be drunk. Not now.

At six, I tiptoed into the bedroom to wake Judy up as promised. She lay there, fully dressed, beneath a blue flowered quilt, her face relaxed and angelic with the tiny suggestion of a smile at the corners of her mouth. I wondered what she was dreaming about to cause her such peace.

Gently, so as not to alarm her, I shook her shoulder and whispered her name. She came awake instantly, her eyes going wide with panic. Then she saw me and relaxed.

"Oh, it's you," she said, rubbing the sleep from her eyes. For some stupid reason, it bothered me that she was able to dismiss my presence with such casual ease. But then I reminded myself we were nothing more than friends and working partners—not lovers with deep emotional ties— and I felt better.

I found some eggs in her kitchen, along with half a pound of bacon. While Judy showered and changed clothes, I fixed breakfast for the two of us. We ate quickly, not talking. Ten minutes later I was standing in front of the building watching her drive away. As she left, I wondered if I would ever see her again. This possibility bothered me profoundly. I had become so close to her, so attached, that I didn't think I could handle not having her around. She was an indispensable asset in the bookstore. But more importantly, she had developed into a crucial part of my personal life. Resultantly, she had etched a permanent place in my heart. I assured myself she'd return in no time.

Back upstairs in the apartment, I found myself ever more impassioned to overcome whatever jarring and deadly but inescapable imminence had cooled my heels. Before blowing my stack, I figured I had to tend to my responsibilities first. With this in mind, I proceeded to call my clerks, starting with Molly. I told her Judy had to take some time off to visit her sister who was sick and that I was unavoidably prevented from coming into the store for the next several days. I told her I'd see to it that all the girls would get a bonus if they carried on without the two of us during our absence. She, I explained, would be in charge. She agreed eagerly. I delightfully boggled myself with how sensible I'd grown. Perhaps the slightest silver lining that had emerged through this upheaval was my strengthening intuition and sharper instincts. Although I had every reason to go off the deep end, I was instead learning to become more grounded and incisive in the midst of disarray.

I called the other girls, and they all agreed as well. Then I dialed Randy's number once more. I could no longer put off knowing what was going on. His phone was answered halfway through the first ring. This time I recognized the voice on the other end instantly.

"Hello. Who is this?"

"Randy," I almost screamed, "it's Carl. Are you all right?"

"Yeah, sure, I'm fine," he said. "Carl, where are you? I've been frantic."

"But you were shot," I said.

"No, I wasn't," he said. "The gorilla missed me. I tripped before he fired at me and knocked myself out on the coffee table. But I don't think he missed by very much. I found a tear in my shirt sleeve. Anyway…" He took a deep breath. "I'm all right. Now, where are you?"

I told him.

"Wait there. I'll be there as fast as I can make it."

Fifteen minutes later, siren blaring and blue lights flashing, a patrol car pulled up in front of the building. Through the window of the apartment, I saw Randy emerge from the passenger side of the car. He was outside the door almost before I could cross the room and open it. He looked at me for about two seconds, then wrapped his arms around me in a tight, passionate hug of relief. After kissing me quickly and tenderly, he let me go. "Come on; we're getting out of here."

"Why the lights and siren?" I asked as we descended to the street.

"I figured if anyone else had found out where you were, the noise would scare them off."

He opened the back door of the squad car for me and climbed back in the front next to the driver, a middle-aged officer in uniform. "Downtown, Harry," he said.

We drove off quickly, but with the lights and siren mercifully turned off. Twenty minutes later, I found myself in the police infirmary for the second time in twenty-four hours while the police surgeon tended to the wound on my face. He put in three stitches at the top of the gash near the cheekbone, pulled the lower part together with two butterfly bandages, and swabbed the whole thing with gauze and adhesive tape. My face felt like the aftermath of the Second World War.

Then, for good measure, he gave me a tetanus booster, which was half again as embarrassing as it was painful. I doubted I would sit comfortably for the next week.

Randy and I went upstairs after that to an office on a restricted floor, where he managed two cups of coffee from somewhere. There was a large brass ashtray on the desk, so I lit a cigarette and settled down in one of the three chairs in the room. Randy took the one behind the desk. The only other furniture consisted of a metal three-drawer filing cabinet and an upright wooden coatrack. I hadn't seen one of those in years.

"I've had some people do some checking while we waited to hear from you," Randy said. He lit a cigarette of his own and leaned back in the swivel chair. "We've come up with some interesting facts."

"Such as?" I tapped ashes into the brass tray.

"Such as," he said, "the fact that John Brunner was born and raised on the island of Kodiak up in Alaska. His father, Horst Brunner, and his young bride, Olga, emigrated from Canada in late 1946. But the interesting part"—he paused to emphasize what he was about to say, taking a sip of coffee from the Styrofoam cup he held in his hand—"is that Horst and Olga Brunner immigrated into Canada in late 1944. And you'll never guess from where."

I hesitated for about a tenth of a second and then said, "From Germany."

"That's right. By way of Denmark. How'd you know?"

I smiled weakly, feeling the muscles draw on the side of my face. "Seemed like a logical guess."

"So," he continued, ignoring my sarcasm, "John was born in Kodiak in 1948. That makes him twenty-seven. His twenty-eighth birthday will fall on June seventeenth of next year. That's just seventeen days before the bicentennial."

"That's all very interesting," I said, "but I fail to see the relevance of John Brunner's birthday to the problem at hand."

Randy favored me with another of his radiant smiles. "I could be wrong, but I've developed a theory."

My eyebrows went back up in mock surprise. "Well, don't keep me sitting here in suspense. Tell me all about it."

And he did, in detail, with all his lines of reasoning. And I must admit the conclusions he had reached seemed valid enough.

Simplified, his theory was this: If John Brunner was indeed Adolf Hitler's son, and if Hitler was still alive, in Kodiak or elsewhere, then it seemed reasonable to assume that a new rise of the Nazi Party would be scheduled for the earliest possible moment.

Why had it taken them this long to accomplish it?

No answer. Not enough data, assuming that a new Nazi Party was their goal. Assuming that Hitler was still alive in the first place and that John Brunner was his son.

But if a neo-Nazi party was scheduled to emerge, what better time to spring it to accomplish a political coup of some sort than on the day of the nation's two hundredth birthday. It would hold great significance in later historical records, and it would provide immense psychological assistance at the immediate moment.

It made sense.

And it provided as good an answer as any to the question of why Brunner was so desperate to get his hands on the birth certificate. He'd need it in order to make any claim to being Adolf Hitler's son and therefore the rightful heir to the title of Führer. Without the document, his claims would be looked upon as just so much hot air.

"So," I said, after he'd outlined it for me and I'd agreed with him that his theories were at least plausible, "what do we do now? Arrest Brunner and make him talk?" I was hoping he'd say yes.

"It might be worth it if we knew where he was," Randy said. "Unfortunately, he seems to have gone to ground somewhere. He hasn't been in his office for the last two days. Nor has he shown up at his home during that time. From what we've been able to learn, that's not especially unusual behavior for our young empire builder, but it does tend to make it difficult to talk to him. Anyway, we have no grounds for his arrest in the first place."

I frowned at him angrily. "What do you mean no grounds? His henchmen tore my house to ribbons. Some of his goons tried to run me off the road. One of them held me at gunpoint on two different occasions. One of them *shot* at you. He's threatened me over the telephone. *And* he hacked my cat to pieces and sent it to me in a plastic bag with a threatening note. If those aren't grounds, tell me what are."

I could feel my cheeks flaming from my uncharacteristic outburst.

"I sympathize, believe me," Randy assured me. "But where's your proof that Brunner was behind any of that? I'll grant you that he probably was. Privately, I'd stake my professional reputation on it. But where's your proof?"

Before I could protest, he started ticking points off on his fingers.

"In the first place, no one saw who tore your house apart. Nor were there any fingerprints. So no proof that Brunner was involved.

"In the second place, you didn't get a good look at the men in the car that chased you onto the freeway—so again, no proof that would tie Brunner to it.

"In the third place, although some of the men—including the one who held the gun on you—who were in my apartment tonight have been identified as employees of Brunner Imports, that doesn't prove they were working with either Brunner's knowledge or consent. And we no longer have them for questioning."

"What about the phone threats?" I asked.

"Anyone can call on the telephone and tell you he's anyone. Even if you recognize the voice, you can't prove it's who you claim it to be. And the same goes for the typewritten note you received with your cat.

"Now, the best we can do is bring him in for questioning about his employees. But we can't arrest him. Not without more information. Not without some proof."

He sighed wearily. "And then, of course, we have to find him before we can bring him in."

I stubbed out my cigarette and reached for my coffee. "All right, what *do* we do, then?"

"We take a little trip up to Victoria." He smiled. "That's what we do."

I must have looked plainly idiotic as my mouth dropped open. "Victoria?" I managed to spit out. "Why Victoria?"

"Because we're overworked and need a break," he said. "And there's someone up there we need to talk to. So we'll kill two birds with one stone."

Realizing what he'd just said, he stopped smiling.

"Figuratively speaking, of course."

16

_— C⚜D —_

ALTHOUGH NOWHERE NEAR AS large as Vancouver, Victoria was the largest city on the island of Vancouver, and as such was the island's chief port and major commercial center. It was the home of the Dominion Astrophysical Observatory and the Royal Canadian Naval Barracks. Its industries included sawmills, woodworking plants, canning, grain elevators, and cold storage plants. It was also the home of one of the finest deep-sea fishing fleets in the world. A residential city with fine scenery, mild climate, and beautiful parks, it was also a tourist city of some note, reveling in old-world charm and sophistication.

In all the years I'd lived in Seattle, I had never availed myself of the opportunity of visiting either Victoria or Vancouver, or anywhere else north of the border. It was just like all the years I'd lived so close to Philadelphia and had never taken the opportunity to attend a concert by the Philadelphia Orchestra, even though they were my favorite recording group. Thinking about it in that context that morning gave me a momentary pang of guilt, just as it did whenever I thought about what I'd left behind in Philadelphia unattended.

Still, I was looking forward to seeing Victoria. Had it not been for the bizarre circumstances that impelled us to go, I would have been more eager to visit. As it was, a tiny cloud of apprehension hung over me as we drove.

We'd drunk more tepid vending machine coffee before setting out, and that hadn't improved my spirits any. We left the building by way of the basement parking garage in a nondescript brown sedan Randy had borrowed for the occasion. It belonged to a Sergeant Yates, and he drove the car out of the garage while Randy and I huddled down in the back seat under a blanket. We stayed under the blanket all the way out to the Big Boy restaurant at 145th and Aurora, where Yates's partner was waiting for us in a patrol car. All precautions Randy had taken to ensure that we weren't followed.

Yates and his partner left to go on patrol, and Randy and I settled down in a booth to drink still more coffee. Now, I like coffee as much as the next man, but halfway through our second cups, I realized Randy was drinking his in an effort to wake himself up. Then it dawned on me—he'd been up all night, just as I had. But it seemed to have caught up with him more severely than it had me.

"Randy," I said, laying my hand on his wrist, "no offense meant, but I think I'm in better shape to drive than you are."

He looked up at me from his half-empty cup, and I noticed for the first time that his eyes were dull and bloodshot. My own probably didn't look much better, and I could feel the first queasy sensations that came with prolonged lack of sleep. But I knew with certainty that if I didn't drive, we might not make it at all. At least with me driving, we probably had a fifty-fifty chance. I was all ready to lay out my string of arguments to combat his protests. To my surprise, he merely nodded his head and slid the car keys across the table to me.

Again, on the off chance that we might be spotted at the main ferry terminal downtown, Randy had laid out a route that would take us up Interstate 5 to Anacortes, where we would board the ferry. I still found it difficult to believe we were being followed by a group with such massive resources that we could be kept under surveillance at every turn, but not so difficult that I argued with Randy's choice of route. While he dozed in the passenger seat, I drove north, chain-smoking to stay awake and listening to the radio turned down low.

We arrived at the ferry terminal a little after eight, paid our fare, and drove on board. I was so tired and edgy by then that I imagined the drivers of all the other cars were conspiring against us. It took a massive effort of will to push the thought out of my mind as a simple paranoid reaction.

A little pamphlet I saw later assured me that our trip from Anacortes to Sidney had been by way of Lopez, Shaw, Orcas Island, and Friday Harbor. But I never saw any of it. I was asleep in my seat almost as soon as the car came to a stop on the ferry. I might have slept the whole day away if one of the crew members hadn't knocked at the car window to wake me and graciously point out that the drivers of the automobiles behind us really would like to depart. Nodding and grumbling to myself as I wiped the sleep out of the corners of my eyes, I engaged the engine and slowly drove off onto the pier.

We had no problems at customs. Randy showed them his badge and informed the immigration officials that we were only going to be in Victoria for the day and that our business was an unofficial inquiry into an official police matter. It seemed to satisfy them, and they let us through.

We stopped in Sidney at a small pastry shop and bought a bag of doughnuts to munch on as we drove down to Victoria. We drove south on BC 17, past the Butchart Gardens, and I might never have known we were not in the United States from the look of the countryside if we hadn't passed a pedestrian overpass stretching blue across the highway. I glanced right as we went under it and noticed a sign with a red hand palm up, which I took to mean that pedestrians should take the overpass instead of crossing the highway.

The few hours of sleep I'd gotten on board the ferry had done me a world of good, and I noticed Randy seemed in better, more alert spirits as well. But, for the most part, we drove in silence until we hit the outskirts of the city. At that point, Randy turned to me and began giving me directions to our destination. It was also at that point that he filled me in on just who it was we were driving up here to see.

His name was Rudolf Gerhardt, and he was one of the city's businessmen who had emigrated from Germany shortly after the war, looking for more fertile opportunities than those we had left in the bombed-out ruins of his homeland. Like Brunner, Gerhardt was involved in the import/export business, among other things. He seemed to have survived the war with most of his fortunes intact, then wasted precious little time doubling and tripling them. In addition to his import/export business, he had money tied up in lumber, real estate, mining, and a small fleet of fishing boats. He was worth, by any conservative estimate, more than I would ever hope to earn in several lifetimes.

He was also the man who had provided the initial capital behind Brunner Imports Ltd., which was what made him important to us. Or so Randy informed me as we threaded the car through the city. Randy reasoned that Gerhardt would never have made that kind of investment without checking on old Horst's background very thoroughly.

"You mean…"

"Exactly," Randy replied. "Even if Gerhardt isn't directly involved with all this, I'd bet my pension he knows most of the details. People like Gerhardt don't get rich—and stay rich—by throwing money away on something they haven't investigated down to the last loose tack."

"Of course," I said, "there might not have been any need for investigation. He might have been in on it from the beginning."

Randy smiled at me grimly. "There's always that, isn't there? I think, when we get there, we'd better be very careful. To that end, I have two undercover lawman's uniforms that you and I will be slipping on. I fabricated a writ that would require any individual to cooperate with officers for an ongoing investigation. I had a colleague in Washington call in ahead of time and set an appointment to confer with Gerhardt, since we'll be arriving incognito."

"You never told me you had this up your sleeve. What if he disregards our appointment and gets caught up with another business matter? This sounds dicey, not to mention very illegal!" I said.

"We'll be breaking several laws, but this might be the only way to secure a meeting with him, Carl. We'll present the court-ordered document to his front desk and demand a meeting for questioning if we have to. You'll just have to trust me and follow my lead."

I remained silent as I thought it through and realized he was right. This was a very busy and important man—we ought to have a legitimate reason for asking to see him. Although I was fazed that he hadn't apprised me of his plan earlier, I found Randy's resourcefulness quite alluring.

Gerhardt's offices were on the eighth floor of a building just several blocks from the historic Empress Hotel. As we had about an hour before our scheduled appointment, Randy suggested we stop in for some of the hotel's famous tea and crumpets. I parked the car a few blocks from the other side of the hotel from Gerhardt's offices, locked the doors, and absentmindedly pocketed the keys.

The Empress was a grand and stately old building of old-world design, covered by red-and-green ivy that clung to the walls as if to shield the hotel with Victorian modesty. The interior, if anything, was more splendid than the exterior. Beautiful dark wooden pillars rose to the vaulted ceilings. Extravagant carved wooden panels and doors surrounded the lobby with muted opulence. The carpeting was thick and lush, and a hushed, reserved tone permeated the atmosphere, almost forcing one to speak in whispers so as not to desecrate it.

The whole forward section of the lobby was arrayed with tables for patrons who had come to observe the traditional teatime. Here and there, people alone and in groups sat awaiting the ancient ritual. Unfortunately, we had arrived much too early. Glancing at his watch, Randy decided we would have to postpone our personal indulgence.

To compensate, we meandered through the lobby and out into the conservatory. The green-mold-covered glass walls rose gracefully to an arched roof. Huge wooden planters overflowed everywhere with greenery. Against the far wall was a wishing well, its sign stating that all money would go to charities that support the disabled and their families.

We observed for about ten minutes and then exited and wandered aimlessly along a pathway that took us by the side of the hotel and back out to the street.

Lighting a cigarette, Randy said, "I suppose we might as well head for Gerhardt's."

I lit a cigarette of my own and followed as he handed me an authentic badge with a phony name to clip on my shirt.

The building in which Gerhardt had his offices could have been a building in any city, anywhere in the world—such was the lack of imagination of most architects. We crossed the lobby, passed the glassed-in building directory that stood in the center of the enclosure looking for all the world like an overly large glass-topped drafting table, and stepped into the self-service elevator. It was one of those with heat-sensitive floor indicators that lit up at a touch from a warm finger. No moving parts! Just cold-blooded, impersonal efficiency.

An unsettling four seconds later, we emerged on the eighth floor, which was occupied in its entirety by Gerhardt's offices. The small alcove off the elevator was dominated by one wall entirely of glass. Simple gold-etched letters above the glass door announced GERHARDT LTD. Beyond the door we could see lush royal-blue carpet on the floors, with four heavy armchairs surrounding a low square modern table, and a profusion of green plants hanging.

We stepped through the door and were greeted by an efficient-looking secretary behind a desk to the right, out of sight of the elevator alcove. Randy announced us and informed her we were expected.

"Good morning, officers. You're a few minutes early," she said in her orderly, impersonal secretary's voice. As hard as she tried, she couldn't hide the trace of British accent that tinged her pronunciation, and I found it rather charming in spite of her aloofness. "However," she continued, "I think Mr. Gerhardt is free. If you'll wait one moment, I'll inform him you're here."

She depressed a button on the intercom console, which, by itself, must have cost more than my automobile, and quietly informed Gerhardt we had arrived. I was unable to hear his reply, which attested to the quality of the intercom system he employed, but it must have been in our favor, for she turned to us and said, "You may go right in." She pointed behind her at the corridor leading away from the reception area.

We thanked her and started walking. We hadn't taken more than four or five steps down the corridor when I thought I heard the sound of a telephone dialing behind me, but it was a fleeting impression, and I dismissed it from my mind.

The last door on the right was not nearly as impressive as I had imagined it would be, and perhaps that spoke for the understated elegance adopted by some of the very rich. Simple black letters on the door spelled out *Gerhardt*. Nothing more. No title. No indication of the importance of the man behind the door in the overall framework of the company. We stepped through and were greeted by a scaled-down version of the reception area: royal-blue carpeting, heavy armchairs, hanging plants, and a grimly efficient-looking secretary behind an immaculate desk.

She rose as we entered. "Officer Neal? Officer Coleman?" Without waiting for a reply, she stepped to the door behind her and opened it. "Mr. Gerhardt is expecting you. You may go right in."

Randy nodded perfunctorily at her, and we allowed ourselves to be ushered into Gerhardt's private office.

I don't know what I was expecting, but it wasn't a tiny, frail-looking man in his seventies. If I'd allowed myself the luxury of a little commonsense reflection, it would have been obvious. Gerhardt, after all, was already a successful businessman at the close of the war. And that was thirty years in the past. Which meant he'd already been a millionaire in his early forties. I couldn't help but admire him for that, despite what he was undoubtedly involved in.

His hair was white, thin, and soft looking, and the pinkness of his scalp shone through in the light from the massive windows behind him. His face was ravaged by age, wrinkled with liver spots. His blue eyes looked vaguely rheumy, moist, almost blank. Fine blue veins showed on the backs of his hands as he stood wearily to greet us, holding out a hand for the traditional amenities.

Randy shook it gently, introduced himself, and then introduced me. While the introductions were in progress, I gazed out the windows at the buildings and the sky beyond. It was an impressive sight.

Gerhardt must have seen the direction of my attention, for he said, "I could have had offices on the top floor. The view from up there, I assure you, is *really* quite extraordinary. But…" He sighed, sitting down in the chair behind his desk. "At the time I thought it would be just a little too ostentatious. I wish now that I had exercised my option. Would either of you care for a drink?"

"Thank you, yes," Randy said.

"If you'd be so kind," he said, his voice an ancient croak. "I'm an old man."

"Certainly," Randy said, looking around him.

Gerhardt touched a button on his desk, and the wall behind and to the right of him lifted silently into the ceiling, revealing a fully stocked wet bar, complete with a refrigerator. "There is a bottle of schnapps, if you would pour me a small touch." He giggled. "My doctor tells me it will kill me if I keep drinking the stuff—but at my age, it doesn't seem to make that much difference, if you know what I mean." It didn't seem to require an answer, nor did he wait for one. "And I'm sure you'll find whatever suits you. Please, help yourselves."

Randy poured about an inch of the schnapps into a glass and carried it to Gerhardt with an almost deferential air. I poured two stiff drinks from a bottle of very old Scotch, added ice cubes from the small freezer, and handed one to Randy. We sat in the two heavy armchairs that flanked the front of the desk.

Gerhardt took an infinitesimal sip of his drink and set the glass down. "Now then," he said, looking at each of us in turn, "how may I help you? The young man who called from Washington wasn't very specific. He only stated that it had something to do with a continuing investigation and that it would be to my advantage to cooperate."

He sat there looking so frail and vulnerable, his eyes going slowly back and forth from my face to Randy's expectantly. I sat there feeling embarrassed, waiting for Randy to forge some kind of opening. Randy sat there sipping his very old Scotch, seemingly lost in thought.

Suddenly he said, "I don't have time to beat around the bush, Gerhardt. We're aware you are affiliated with John Brunner. We have the birth certificate. We want to know what you know about it. If you cooperate, we won't have to cause you any harm. If you don't, I'll exhume all your corrupt and felonious business affairs and personally ensure that you get thrown the book in the hall of justice."

It was as if every muscle in the old man's body went limp at the same time. His shoulders sagged, his jaw dropped, and his hands slumped on the desk in front of him. He aged thirty years in two seconds, looking far closer to a decrepit one hundred than his true age. He sputtered and gasped for air at the same time. Altogether, it was a pathetic sight. And frightening.

I ran to the bar, filled a glass of water from the tap, and carried it to the old man. His hands were too weak to hold it himself, so I ended up holding it for him, and eventually I managed to get several swallows down his throat.

"That was pretty cold blooded," I snarled at Randy as I eased Gerhardt back upright into his chair and loosened his tie and collar. "He's an old man, Randy."

"Sure he's an old man," Randy said, standing up. "But don't let that fool you. He's a crafty old bastard as well. He'd have to be, to have ended up a multimillionaire. And you can bet what's left of that nice little house of yours in Seattle that he'd have played his age for everything it's worth trying to draw us out, possibly making some kind of deal. I had to do it this way, Carl. Hit him hard and fast before he had time to gain the upper hand."

I was ready to offer some arguments in favor of humanitarianism and good old-fashioned decency and fair play when I noticed Gerhardt out of the corner of my eye. He was feebly waving his right hand in my direction. Some of the color had returned to his cheeks, turning them from deathly pale to a healthy ashen tint. Although he looked as if he might just surprise us and live, I couldn't help but think that he looked, still, like a sadly defeated old man.

"He's right, you know," he croaked at me, pointing to Randy. "I would have done just as he said. But I feel a little weak just now. My heart, you know. Not as strong as it once was."

He was gasping for breath between his words, and I told him to rest a minute. But he brushed my concern aside with another wave of his hand.

"No, I must tell you now. If I wait to regain my strength, I just might regain my resolve as well. And I've lived with it too long as it is."

Randy sat back in his chair. Not knowing what else to do, I did likewise. I retrieved my drink from where I'd set it on the desk and took two long swallows, surprised by how much I needed it to calm my nerves.

"I want to know what you know about the birth certificate," Randy said, softly this time, almost painfully. "Is it real? And if it is, what does it mean?"

"It's real enough, all right," Gerhardt told him. "At least, I've never had any reason to doubt its authenticity. You see, I knew the man whose birth certificate it was."

"I thought perhaps you might have," Randy said. "So what does it mean?"

Gerhardt picked up his glass of schnapps and took a sip. I could almost see the alcohol bring the color back to his face. "I will tell you everything I know," he said. "Because I'm certain you aren't bluffing, as I've done my fair share of commercialism by gleaning the benefits of bending the law."

"For what you call bending, any judge would impose on you a life sentence. I can attest to that," Randy snapped.

"You must forgive me," Gerhardt said, "but old men get curious. Our curiosity is about the only thing we have left unsatisfied that we can still do anything about. Age fairly well sees to that. And once our curiosity goes, death is not far behind, even though the body may linger on for years. But I digress. What I would like, if you would be so kind, is for you to tell me how you happened to be in possession of the document. I should have thought it much too safe for such an eventuality."

"That's none of your concern. We will be the ones asking the questions. Tell us what you know, or else!" Randy said.

Gerhardt took another sip of his schnapps and then launched into one of the most amazing tales I had ever heard.

He had been a successful businessman in Germany at the time Adolf Hitler was showing promise of reaching a position of power inside the German government. Several times, he heard Hitler speak to assemblies about his ideology. It seemed natural to him at the time to lend his financial support to Hitler's cause, and he was one of the first German industrialists to do so. Later, once the Third Reich had been firmly established, Hitler saw fit to repay the gesture by giving Gerhardt's business a preferred status. After that, he quickly doubled and redoubled his fortunes.

It was also during that period that he cultivated Hitler's personal friendship. They met often in the early days of the Reich, but never openly. At first, that puzzled Gerhardt. But eventually, Hitler made it clear to him. He was holding Gerhardt in reserve, as part of what Hitler referred to as the Siegfried Contingency. As the months unfolded, it became clear to Gerhardt what the Siegfried Contingency was, and the scope of it only confirmed in his mind the true brilliance and meticulous planning ability of the Führer. He was proud to remain anonymous as the key to Hitler's scheme.

"What you must never forget," Gerhardt said, "was that Adolf Hitler was a genius. He had a plan for world dominance the likes of which had not been seen since the idea first occurred to Alexander the Great. He was a master planner. And as such, he foresaw every eventuality as his plan unfolded—every delay, every snag, every setback, every defeat."

According to Gerhardt, Hitler had only given his initial drive—what became known as World War II—about a 60 percent probability. If it had succeeded, so much the better; the millennium would have been achieved that much sooner. But he never pinned all his hopes on success in the forties. There were too many things against him, the emerging strength and determination of the United States only one factor among all the others.

So he had various contingency plans thought through and prepared for implementation as they became necessary. A few were rough outlines, ready to be filled in and fleshed out as circumstances dictated. But most of them—including the Siegfried Contingency—were fully prepared and ready to launch long before Poland was invaded in 1939.

"One of the strokes of genius of our Führer," Gerhardt continued, his eyes blank, his mind wandering back thirty years, "was his talent for misdirection. A necessary talent for a man in the limelight, you know. For only by misdirection can an instantly recognizable figure hope to walk down a public street unnoticed. Martin Bormann is a perfect example of that."

Martin Bormann, Gerhardt told us, was handpicked by Hitler to lead the Nazi Party in case anything should happen to the Führer. Those surrounding Hitler knew of the arrangement even if most of the general public did not. However, toward the end of the war, when it became apparent to Hitler that this particular thrust was doomed to defeat, he sent Bormann into hiding so he would be in a position to lead the next assault.

In order that those who might try to track Bormann down and destroy him should fail, Hitler launched the Bormann Contingency. It consisted of a carefully planned and flawlessly executed series of leaks regarding Bormann's whereabouts. The leaks were prolific; the sightings, for the most part, impeccable. The genius of the plan was that all the sightings were contradictory. Some had him in Germany, some in France, some in South America, some in Spain, and one even in Egypt. Yet none of them were true. They had all been carefully stage-managed in order to throw would-be pursuers off the track.

"Of course," Gerhardt said, smiling benignly, "history has uncovered this particular plan. As you know, Bormann's bones were finally discovered in Berlin in 1970. He had never left Germany at all.

"What you don't know, however, is that Bormann was a red herring right from the beginning. He was never intended to lead the new Nazi Party."

I came halfway off my chair at that. I remembered Clive Wrenshurst's book so well. In *But for the Mad Hatter*, the professor had made several references to the fact that Bormann had been carefully groomed to succeed Hitler in the eventuality of his death. I respected Wrenshurst's opinion—an opinion shared by many others in positions that would have enabled them to get at the truth of the matter. "You're saying that history is all wrong on this point? I find that hard to accept."

"It would have been a complete failure of the Bormann Contingency if it were easy to accept," Gerhardt said. His cheeks had regained their healthy color, almost as if the talk about his Führer was acting as a powerful stimulant.

Randy settled back into his chair and handed me a fresh drink. Glancing over at him, I saw he had refilled his own glass as well. I hadn't even noticed him getting out of his chair.

"Don't you see?" Gerhardt said. "Hitler was presumed dead in the bunker. Also a carefully stage-managed performance. Bormann—the chosen successor—on the run, no one knowing precisely where. The threat of a neo-Nazi party rising from the ashes of the Third Reich imminent. The solution? Find Bormann and cut him down, thus stopping the emergence of a new Nazi threat. Or, at the very least, seriously slowing it down."

There were many people, Gerhardt went on, who lived in great fear of a reemergence of the Nazi Party. It had been so persuasive once—had caused so much terror and destruction, so much loss of life. For it to ever happen again had to be prevented at all costs. This, he explained, was the true motivation of people such as the famed Nazi hunter Simon Wiesenthal and others like him. True, revenge was a prominent secondary motive. But, first and foremost, they wanted to find the escaped Nazi leaders and eliminate them so they would never be in a position to spearhead a return of the terror they symbolized.

So, although it was never well publicized, Martin Bormann was the principal target of their searches. He was the heir apparent, and as such, the former Nazis and the neo-Nazis would swarm around him like drones around a queen bee. He had to be found and eliminated at all costs.

"And for twenty-five years, all major efforts were aimed in that direction. For twenty-five years, the Nazi hunters have bent the lion's share of their resources to finding and destroying Martin Bormann, thinking that if they did so, they would have decapitated the beast and rendered it harmless."

Randy lit a cigarette and reached for the brass ashtray on Gerhardt's desk. "And now you're telling us that it was all a smoke screen?"

"Precisely," Gerhardt said. "You see, for twenty-five years, everyone has been looking in the wrong direction. For twenty-five years, no one has ever suspected the truth. Oh, a few have conjectured that it was not Hitler who died in the bunker. But almost no one took them seriously. And even if they did, they did not guess at what it might mean if it was true. For, you see, the scope of the Siegfried Contingency was too vast, too glorious, too imbued with the Führer's genius for such little minds to grasp it."

"Perhaps you should explain this Siegfried Contingency to us," Randy said. "Obviously, it has something to do with the twin brother."

"Oh, absolutely," Gerhardt said. "In fact, it was conceived on the basis of the fact that Adolf Hitler had an identical twin the world knew nothing about."

Hitler's twin brother, Gerhardt told us, had been born mentally incapacitated. He was somehow unable to grasp the difference between fantasy and reality. He proved to be a great embarrassment and shame to the family. So, at the age of four, he was left in the care of a private institution under his mother's maiden name. From that day on, he was never mentioned outside the family again.

Young Adolf, of course, grew up knowing about his brother and the secret shame he had brought on the family. He was told that, as far as the neighbors and townsfolk knew, young Siegfried had died. He was also told how lucky he was to have been spared a similar fate and that someday he should strive to achieve greatness to help atone for the sins that had caused his brother to be born abnormal. Which might have, Gerhardt concluded, had an influence on both his later hatred of Christianity and the Jewish religion from which it sprang and on his decision to rid the world of inferior beings and make it a paradise of perfect specimens. That, of course, was pure conjecture on his part, based on nothing concrete.

"You mean," I asked, not sure I had grasped the point, "that Hitler saw his twin brother condemned to insanity because of some burden of sin imposed on him by Christianity? And because he couldn't accept that verdict, he rejected the Christian religion as well?"

"Precisely," Gerhardt said. "And the Jewish religion, as the Jews were the inferior people who had spawned the Christian belief, no matter how inadvertently. In fact, I think he held the Jews even more guilty than the Christians, because had there not been any Jews, Christianity would never have existed."

"And you call this line of reasoning the product of a rational mind?" Randy asked.

"Rationality is a matter of opinion," Gerhardt said defensively. "One man's rationality is another man's nonsense. And besides, who can be rational when he is discussing religion? It is, at best, an irrational subject." He held up one finger on his right hand, indicating he had just thought of another point. "And, you must remember, these were opinions young Adolf formulated when he was a very young boy. Such inbred beliefs, especially when they are instilled at a very young age, are often most difficult to dislodge.

"However, it matters not how he arrived at the opinion. There were many of us who agreed with it, even if we arrived at our belief on a different route. There is, you know, often more than one path to the truth."

"All very interesting, I'm sure," I said, "but I think we are drifting away from the point."

Gerhardt's eyes lit up. He picked up his drink and took another sip, reminding me of the one I still held in my hand. I took a swallow, set it on the desk, and reached into my pocket for a cigarette I didn't really want except as something to keep my nervous hands occupied.

"Yes, well," Gerhardt went on, "as I said, the Führer was a meticulous planner. He foresaw numerous eventualities. He even foresaw the possibility that his thrust toward the perfect world order would be defeated by the overwhelming numbers of his inferior opposition.

"Knowing that the Third Reich would need strong leadership, should it be defeated, in order to reemerge at a more propitious time, he formulated the Siegfried Contingency to ensure his own survival. Not that he was a particularly egotistic man, for he wasn't. He was, instead, very practical. He recognized within himself the charismatic qualities of a true leader. It was these very qualities that led him to the position of undisputed ruler of Germany, buoyed up by a wave of fanatical popular support. And it was these very qualities, this very popularity, that would be needed to lead the Nazi Party out of temporary defeat and into the victory history had outlined for it.

"Of course, Hitler couldn't merely announce his retirement as if he were the head of some giant corporation. He had too many enemies, too many people in influential places who saw his movement as other than it truly was and felt he should be punished. And he knew this would be the case. The inferior species, like cancerous cells in the body, would never acknowledge their own inferiority. They would never willingly submit to their surgical removal. Instead, they would fight back, fanatically, for their right to survive."

"And you don't think these people had a right to survive?" I asked him.

Gerhardt frowned at me like an impatient parent might frown at a child who was being deliberately obtuse. "No more right to survive than cancer has. You cut off a gangrenous leg in order to save the rest of the body, and you don't put it to a vote ahead of time. You simply operate as quickly and efficiently as you can."

"But people aren't some impersonal disease," Randy protested. "They have rights, even if they are in disagreement with your beliefs."

Gerhardt snorted derisively. "I could hardly expect you to understand. As one of your philosophers once put it, 'If you're not part of the solution, you're part of the problem.' And I think that sums it up quite nicely."

"Let's not argue philosophy," I said. "I'd rather hear the rest of this story." I puffed on my cigarette, ground it out, and automatically reached for another.

Gerhardt picked up the story where he'd left off.

In order for Hitler to leave the country unnoticed, he had to do so by misdirection. He used the ultimate misdirection at his disposal: his twin brother, identical in every way except for his mental processes.

Early on in his rise to power, he had his brother stealthily installed in his private quarters. Only his private nurse knew he was there. Food was brought to him surreptitiously, for no one would have been bold enough to speculate where the extra food was going. "Some, I'm sure, furtively thought he had a secret mistress." Gerhardt chuckled.

Hitler spent much time with his brother, teaching him the things he would need to know—convincing him, in fact, that he himself was actually Adolf Hitler, Chancellor of Germany, Führer of the Third Reich. All in the eventuality that one day he would be needed to serve the cause in his peculiar, singular capacity to do so.

"What would have happened to the brother if Hitler had been successful?" I asked, unable to restrain myself.

"Why, he would have been quietly eliminated," Gerhardt said. "Just as his nurse was, shortly prior to Hitler's departure from Germany."

The simple declaration of the fact of the nurse's death drove home again the ruthlessness of the man we were discussing. It knotted up my stomach and brought bile to the back of my throat.

"Late in 1944," Gerhardt went on, "the Führer saw the imminent collapse of the war. But he didn't panic. As I told you, he had only given the war a sixty percent probability of success. He knew, from the very beginning, that the world might not be ready—or worthy—of his dream. So he put the Siegfried Contingency into effect."

Plans had already been meticulously laid for Hitler's secret departure from Germany. He left in the middle of the night aboard a submarine with a handpicked crew of men who were fanatical in their loyalty to him. Men who were sworn to secrecy concerning the precious cargo they carried. Along with Hitler, they also carried Gerta Brodl, Hitler's longtime secret lover. Gerta Brodl was also devoted to the Führer, and she was a perfect specimen of womanhood in his eyes. The perfect woman to bear him a son and heir.

I sat and listened in stupefied wonder as the tale unfolded, scarcely able to believe my ears, unable to tear myself away from the logic of it.

The submarine sailed at great depth, avoiding all known Allied shipping lanes, several times narrowly escaping detection by American antisubmarine patrols. Eventually, it reached a point on the deserted coast of Kodiak Island in Alaska. There, Hitler and Gerta were put ashore in the dead of the night. They made their way to the home of Gerta's older sister, who had established residence on the island long before the war, at Hitler's direction. With the aid of forged papers and false immigration entry forms, they joined the community as the older sister's newly arrived Austrian relatives. They were accepted into the community in no time at all.

"Naturally," Gerhardt told us, "Hitler had made changes to his appearance. His moustache was gone, and his hair was cropped very short. He took to wearing his reading glasses in public. He looked almost nothing at all like his pictures in the newspapers and newsreels. One would have, in fact, needed reason for suspicion first in order to begin looking for similarities."

But all possible suspicion had been removed ahead of time by the fact that Hitler—in the guise of his twin brother—was still in Germany, at the helm of the Nazi ship of state.

Nor was the reliability of the submarine crew left to chance. Hitler had chosen the captain well, a fanatic's fanatic. He alone, of his crew, knew the facts. Halfway back to Germany, somewhere in the mid-Atlantic, the captain triggered a preset series of mines that ran down the underbelly of the submarine. Subsequent reports of German ships discovered after the war confirmed that this particular submarine was lost at sea and never heard of again.

"You mention this woman, Gerta Brodl," Randy said. "I thought it was fairly common knowledge that Eva Braun was Hitler's mistress."

"Another deception, I'm afraid," Gerhardt said. "Eva was passionately devoted to Hitler. She was very much in love with him. So much in love with him, in fact, that she willingly agreed to sacrifice herself in order to give credibility to the overall deception. She carried on with the twin, Siegfried, as though he were the very man he had always been. It would have been suspicious, naturally, if she had shunned him at the time when people needed to know more than ever that it was the same man.

"Actually"—he chuckled—"her marriage to Hitler in the bunker was rather a nice touch, don't you think? And obviously her own idea."

"It's incredible," Randy said. "It's almost too much to be believed."

"You can believe it," Gerhardt said, "for it is all quite, quite true."

17

RANDY GOT UP AND began pacing around the office, clearly agitated by what he had heard. In spite of everything that had just transpired, I couldn't help but revel in the superb motion of his body as he moved. I could see the muscles of his legs against the material of his slacks. His chest and arms fought against the thin cloth of his shirt, and in my mind's eye, I could see him once again as he was without the artificial barrier of clothing.

He shattered my daydream by saying, "This is all very good and interesting, Herr Gerhardt. Especially if it *is* true. And, for the sake of argument, I will grant you your story's validity. With the existence of the birth certificate to back it up, I must admit it makes both logical and historical sense.

"I know that at the end of 1944, for instance, Adolf Hitler underwent a severe personality change. Many of those closest to him couldn't find any reasonable explanation for it. It was almost as if he had become an entirely different person. Your story would explain it.

"What I don't understand, however, is your role in all this. I believe you said you were to be the key to the so-called Siegfried Contingency, did you not? In what way, if I may ask?"

Gerhardt gave him a tolerant smile from behind his desk. He looked like an old-fashioned schoolmaster trying to deal with an insubordinate student who was deliberately failing to grasp the point.

"Why, for money of course," he said. "The Fourth Reich had to be built on something. The Führer surmised—and rightly so, I think you'll agree—that his ability to draw credit would be severely limited." He laughed at his own sarcastic remark. "I had much money at the time, most of it acquired by favor of the Führer. It was only natural that I return some of it to its rightful source."

He went on to explain that with the money he had and was able to remove from Germany with Hitler's personal help, he emigrated from Germany to Switzerland in mid-1944. Shortly after the war, with his tracks covered completely, he applied for and was granted immigration status in Canada. There, he founded the business empire he currently controlled. Not only was he in an excellent position to disperse his own money for the cause, but his empire became the perfect clearinghouse for other hordes of Nazi Party money that had been removed from Germany before its collapse. And, although he was not directly involved in this part of it, his various businesses and international interests made perfect clearinghouses for information as well.

"So, Adolf Hitler of Germany became Horst Brunner of Austria, relocated in Alaska during the war. He was a simple man, apparently living on the charitable contributions of his new wife's sister. A year after they were married, she bore him a son. And, of course, they lived on an income secretly supplied to them by me.

"Later, when young Johann Brunner came to me with the idea of opening a business in the United States, I was most eager and pleased to put up the capital for his venture. He assured me the United States was the logical place from which to stage his bid for power as the son of Adolf Hitler and rightful heir to the title of Führer. If the United States, the world's powerhouse, could be infected from the inside out, the resurrection of the Nazi Party would be more impactful than if any other country was inflicted."

I shook my head in wonder, and not a little bit in bitter disgust at the obvious pride with which this frail old man told of his part in the scheme.

"You are telling us, then," Randy asked, "that we are to believe John Brunner of Brunner Imports Limited is actually the son of Adolf Hitler?"

"I have given you the facts as I know them to be true. Whether you believe them is up to you." He glared at us, as if defying us to call him a liar.

"All right," Randy said wearily, "assuming again that everything you have told us is true, what are Brunner's plans?"

"I've told you enough," the old man said. "In fact, more than I ever should have." He waved a hand at us imperiously. "I'm tired now. I wish you to leave me."

Randy rounded the desk before I had time to comprehend his movements. He had the old man's collar clenched in his hand and the frail old body halfway up out of its seat with his pistol viciously shoved up under Gerhardt's nose before I had time to formulate a protest. I started to say something, and Randy snarled. "Shut up and stay out of this!"

I sank back in my chair, stupefied, both at his vicious physical assault on the old man and his curt, unfeeling tone toward me.

"I'll give you ten seconds to continue talking," Randy said to him, "and then I'm going to blow your head off."

I gasped but refrained from commenting.

Gerhardt looked weary and said, "Go ahead and kill me. I'm an old man. I've been living on borrowed time for a long time. Death ceased to frighten me a long time ago. I will go to my grave a contented man knowing of my contribution to the glory of the master race. You can't take that away from me. Besides, nothing I have told you matters anymore; it's too late to stop the plan that's been set in motion."

Randy stood there for ten seconds, his finger growing white against the trigger of his weapon, and for a fleeting moment, I actually thought he was going to carry out his threat. Then, disgustedly, he shoved the old man back into the chair and reholstered his gun.

Walking around the desk, he suddenly spun back and said, "You're wrong there, Gerhardt. I *can* take that away from you. I can reduce you to the traitor you are in the eyes of your slimy little Nazi cohorts."

"No," he said wearily, "you couldn't do that. How could you?"

"It wouldn't be hard," Randy said. "I have influential friends in Washington. Influential enough to get this story published all across the country. And believe me, a story of this magnitude would soon be in circulation all around the globe. I would be very sure you got all the credit as the source of our information. In the eyes of every Nazi and Nazi sympathizer on the face of the earth, you would be viewed as a traitor to the party. You would be dirt. Your name would be spit out in disgust. Your memory would be blotted out of the annals of Nazi history as if it never existed."

I sat there in horrid fascination, watching Gerhardt's body sinking in his chair, shriveling before the onslaught of Randy's verbal lashing. Finally, his eyes horror struck at the picture that had been presented to him, he held up his hands, palms out—the universal gesture of surrender. "Stop," he croaked. "For God's sake, stop."

"Then tell me what I want to know," Randy demanded.

"And if I do?"

"Our source of information will remain a closely guarded secret. You will be allowed to live out your life with your complicity unrevealed."

"You mean you'll let me go, a free man?" he asked, his eyes opening in disbelief.

"Don't be naïve," Randy said. "Of course you will be taken into custody. Before this day is out, I'm afraid. That decision will be out of my hands in any case. But if you cooperate, your memory will go untarnished."

Gerhardt sat there, weighing his options.

"It's the best I can do," Randy said. "Take it or leave it."

Finally, Gerhardt raised his head. "All right. I'll tell you what you want to know."

Randy retrieved his drink and sat back down, ready to listen. I felt a thin thread of disgust blossoming in my stomach and lit a cigarette to try to stem it.

"There is a group of men in your country," Gerhardt began, "that is very influential in the American political scene. Not well known, you understand. In fact, I myself do not know their identities. But they do exist, and they are very powerful.

"Johann has approached them with the truth. They were very receptive to it, and they've made plans to support him as a dark-horse candidate for the presidency of the United States in this year's elections. They have chosen this year for its psychological implications. Everyone is gearing up to celebrate the bicentennial. Their plan is for Johann to announce his plans to campaign for the presidency on July Fourth, the nation's two hundredth birthday. They have a comprehensive platform prepared, one that will be met with great approval by a great many people in your country. People who are tired of the same worn-out promises that are never delivered.

"At the same time he announces his candidacy, he will also reveal his true identity. This group of men who stand behind him feel it will be nothing but an asset. Every splinter socialist group in the nation will rally in his support. His victory could be overwhelming, for there are many people who are sympathetic to much of what the socialists stand for, despite the fact that they have never openly chosen to join a socialist political group."

"But in order for it to work," Randy said, "Brunner will have to come up with the birth certificate to prove he is who he claims."

"Exactly," Gerhardt said. "And I must warn you, you were in very grave danger before you came here. Your lives are of no consequence to them. Now, should they ever discover that you know the truth, your lives will be worthless. You will be hunted down and slaughtered like mad dogs."

His eyes were blazing with fury. Slowly, he began to stand up from his chair. "And now, I have told you all I know. I have business to attend to before I am taken away. So, if you would be so kind as to excuse me—"

The window behind him erupted in a shower of glass, and his frail old body was slammed forward across his desk with the force of a felled tree.

Randy and I hit the floor in an almost simultaneous motion. In a flash of movement, Randy was across the room and kneeling beneath the shattered window, his pistol clenched tightly in his hand. "Stay down," he shouted.

The door behind us opened, and Gerhardt's secretary came running in. She took one look and screamed. "Get back!" I shouted at her, but she was beyond hearing. Still screaming, she rushed across the room to where her employer lay across his desk.

No shots rang out, and she was a perfect target.

A few minutes crept by, the secretary still screaming like a siren gone berserk. Finally, Randy said, "Shut her up, will you?"

I crab walked across the floor, grabbed her arm at the elbow, and pulled her to the floor beside me. The sudden movement failed to stifle her screams, so I covered her mouth with my hand.

She stopped screaming.

Across the room, Randy was edging his head over the shattered windowsill. He looked across the expanse toward the neighboring buildings for what seemed like a very long time, though it was probably less than a minute. Finally, he stood up.

"I guess they got who they were after," he said.

"Presumably before he told us what he knew," I added. I was still holding the secretary by the arm. I let it drop by her side and stood up. "But how did they know…" I suddenly remembered the receptionist and what I'd thought had sounded like a telephone dialing.

"The receptionist!" I cried, racing for the office door. But, as I should have expected, her desk was empty by the time I got there. I returned to Gerhardt's office somewhat more sedately. Randy was bending over the old man's body.

"He's dead," he announced solemnly. "I've already called the police."

We waited for the police to arrive. Randy gave them the official story about an investigation into some illegal and possibly treasonous activities of an American national. He was at a loss to explain why someone would have wanted Gerhardt dead, unless it was to keep him from revealing potentially damaging information. And no, he told them in response to their inevitable question, Gerhardt had revealed nothing that might have been worth killing him to prevent its leaking out. He could have been on the verge, but Randy wasn't sure.

It took some time before all the red tape was sorted out, and in the end, Randy had to give them a name and telephone number in Washington in order to get us out of there. We waited patiently while they made the call. When they finished, they told us we were free to go.

The sky had darkened by the time we left, and the first spatters of an approaching rainstorm were already hitting the streets. Neither of us felt like returning to the Empress for the tea and crumpets we'd promised ourselves, so we found a coffee shop and settled for cups of coffee we really didn't want either.

By the time we were ready to catch the ferry back to Seattle, the rain was coming down in sheets. We raced frantically to the car. Since I had the keys in my pocket, I automatically slipped into the driver's seat. I opened Randy's door for him, and once he was inside, he made no protest to me at the wheel.

I eased the car away from the curb into the darkness and the downpour and headed for the ferry terminal. We were both so lost in our private thoughts that neither of us noticed the nondescript sedan when it pulled out behind us.

18

NEITHER OF US NOTICED the car after we were aboard the ferry, either, and we blithely went about settling in for the cruise down to Seattle without an inkling of the danger that lay ahead of us. Once we'd parked the car and locked it securely, we went up to the passenger deck to get a cup of coffee.

"It doesn't make sense that they would kill Gerhardt and not one of us," Randy said, his hands wrapped around his mug of steaming coffee. His clothes were as damp and cold as my own, so he must have been at least as uncomfortable as I was. But, unlike me, his mind was on the case rather than his own comfort.

I pushed my attention away from the clinging fabric that was irritating the backs of my thighs where it chafed against the chair, trying to focus on his line of thinking. "It does make sense in a way," I said. "Gerhardt had served his useful purpose. He provided the monies necessary for Brunner and his gang to initiate their plan and carry it toward its conclusion. According to Gerhardt, that conclusion isn't far off."

Randy started to say something, but I held up my hand to ward him off. "No, let me finish." He shrugged, so I went on. "OK, if we assume Gerhardt has outlived his usefulness, that means *we* are still useful to them in some way. Which is, of course, the birth certificate. Don't you see? They dare not get rid of us until they have it back in their possession."

He sipped at his coffee and set the cup down. "That explains why they didn't kill you when they had the chance. But not me. I don't have their document. And they must realize by now that I represent some threat to them."

I colored a little with embarrassment as the realization hit me. Back in Randy's apartment, I had not only told them Randy worked for a supersecret group in Washington, but I'd hinted quite strongly that it was Randy and not myself who held the secret of the certificate's whereabouts.

"Randy," I said, looking up at him painfully.

He didn't look up from his coffee. "What is it?"

"Randy, I'm sorry, but I think I tipped them to the group you work for."

He looked up then, his eyes wide and bright. "You what?"

So I explained it to him. And when I'd finished telling him that I thought he was dead at the time and that I had made up a story in order to save my own skin, I sat back and reached for my shirt pocket, hunting for a cigarette—my eyes never leaving his face.

A few minutes later, his eyes softened, and his right hand reached across the narrow table to grasp my left wrist. He squeezed it gently and gave me a weary smile. "Don't blame yourself, Carl. These things happen. If the situation had been reversed, I probably would have done the same thing."

I smiled back at him, a wave of relief flowing over me. The last thing I wanted at the moment was to lose his respect. And, yes, his love. Selfish of me, I suppose, but that was the way I felt.

My hand came away from my pocket empty. I had left my cigarettes below in the car. "Randy, do you have a cigarette? I think I could really use one."

He patted his pockets and then said, "No. I'm out, remember? I was smoking yours the last few miles."

I did remember. In fact, that was why they weren't in my pocket; I'd laid them on the seat between us so he could help himself.

Randy started to stand up. "I'll go buy a pack."

"At the prices they charge on this scow!" I said in mock outrage, trying to reintroduce a sense of levity I did not feel. "Don't be ridiculous. I've got almost half a pack down in the car. It'll only take me a moment to get them."

I was out of my seat and halfway to the door that led down to the vehicle deck before he could protest. Glancing over my shoulder as I reached the door, I saw him resignedly resuming his seat and reaching for his coffee. I resolved at that point to treat him to a very long vacation when this was all over.

Moments later, I was sitting in the driver's seat, one leg dangling out the door, my left foot on the deck, reaching across the seat to where the cigarettes had apparently slid when Randy had left the car.

I glanced up at the rearview mirror, and that was when I noticed the nondescript sedan that had followed us.

Or, more correctly, that was when I noticed the two men who were quickly emerging from the vehicle. Their sudden movements had caught my attention, and when I looked at them again, I noticed details. They were both large and muscular looking, and the expressions on their faces were not the kind usually associated with friendly social intercourse. In fact, their lips were drawn back tightly in hideous, sadistic grins, giving them an appearance of almost pure evil.

That in itself was enough to make my blood stop flowing. But immediately following my appraisal of their faces, I noticed what they held in their hands. Both men carried dark, heavy pistols in their right hands, and even from that distance, the shapes could easily be recognized for what they were: long-barreled, sinister-looking German Luger semiautomatics. I had been confident our pursuers needed to keep us alive, but from the murderous looks on their faces, doubt rapidly ensued.

My heart leaped to my throat, and for a moment I thought I would panic into immobility. Then, some buried instinct for survival spurred me into action. I lurched out of the car and started running for the door that led back up to the passenger deck.

The neatly ordered rows of cars and trucks lined up on the vehicle deck proved to be both a blessing and a curse. By ducking down behind the nearest car and moving forward in a scrabbling crab walk, I was able to avoid a clear line of fire for my pursuers. On the other hand, the automobiles prevented me from racing in a direct line for the stairwell. And the moment I ducked, I lost sight of the two gunmen.

Inching along in a half-stooped position, I slowly made my way toward the hatch leading up to other people and relative safety. My movements were hampered by the fact that I couldn't poke my head up to see what progress I'd made for fear of having it blown off by one of Brunner's trigger-happy henchmen. Next time, I thought irrelevantly, I would allow Randy to pay any price he wanted for a pack of cigarettes.

I ducked down lower and peered beneath the wheels of the parked cars. My objective was only one row away, across a short clearing left vacant for the passengers to move freely in and out of the doorway. I had only to inch my way around the car I was crouched behind, race across the clearing, and dash through the door up the steps.

I recalled that the door was on some sort of pneumatic hinge and, unfortunately, wouldn't open all that quickly. So I had no doubt that one or both of the gunmen would have more than sufficient time to drop me where I stood before I could reach safety.

I moved my head in the other direction and saw a pair of well-polished feet standing on the deck behind the car to my rear. My heart started again. I hadn't realized they were that close.

I was about to stand up and surrender, hoping I would find a better opportunity for escape at a later time, when I heard the door to the stairwell wheeze open. Glancing back to my right, I saw a familiar pair of feet emerging.

"Randy, get down!" I yelled, heedless of the danger my outburst might put me in. "There are two of them, and they're both armed!"

I saw the feet scramble madly away from the door and disappear behind a row of cars on the other side of the deck. My ear caught movement behind me, and I turned back in time to see a face peering at me from under the nearest car.

"Stand up slowly," it hissed. "You can't possibly escape." The barrel of the Luger poked out from under the car, aimed directly at my face. There didn't seem much else I could do, under the circumstances, but comply with his order.

As I started to rise, I saw the face move upward behind the car as the gunman started to do likewise. In a moment of sheer inspiration brought on by desperation, I snapped quickly to my feet, placed my hands on the rear side windows of the cars on either side of me, and pushed upward with all my strength. My feet came off the floor, and I twisted my body to the left, swinging my rigid legs in an arc across the trunk of the car. My feet came up above it, knocking the man off balance. He fell heavily back to the deck. My own momentum carried me across the car, and I landed on top of him, one foot coming down on his chest and the other landing squarely on his upturned jaw. I heard the sickening sound of crunching bone.

Desperately, I looked around for his gun, but it was nowhere in sight. Then, realizing I must present a perfect target for the unconscious man's partner, I ducked down between the cars and moved swiftly away.

I stopped two rows over and four cars forward to catch my breath. All around me, the boat deck was silent. For the first time since arriving on the vehicle deck, I became aware of the rain pounding against the sides of the ferry. The vessel was rocking slightly in the storm-tossed waters, and occasional high waves broke over the upraised gate at the end of the deck, sending wavelets sliding along the concrete to form large circular puddles.

The atmosphere was dank and gloomy and foreboding, and the intense silence wasn't helping any.

Finally, I could no longer take not knowing what was going on. I poked my head down and peered beneath the wheels of the cars, but at the angle I was looking, I could see nothing but rows and rows of tires. Off to my right, I could barely make out the outstretched arm of the man I had just felled.

Taking a chance, I stood up for a better view. At first I saw nothing. Then, out of the corner of my eye, I caught a slight movement. Turning my head to see, I witnessed a horrifying scene. Randy was at the extreme stern end of the ferry, near the uplifted gate, facing the port side of the ship where the bulkhead came down to meet the gate. Behind him stood the other gunman, about twenty feet away and behind two rows of cars. His Luger was coming down in a slow arc as he leveled his arm in Randy's direction.

"Randy, behind you. Look out!" I screamed.

Randy whirled around, his own pistol drawn, but the gunman was faster. His Luger spurted flame, and I saw Randy's body flung backward. I cried out and began racing forward as fast as the parked cars would allow me to, unaware my feet had started moving.

But I was too late.

Randy's body hit the retaining wall of the ship, then arced upward and back. I thought I saw his hand grapple at the slippery metal, but I wasn't sure. I only knew his body toppled backward and disappeared over the side into the swirling, storm-tossed water below.

Then, two things happened. The gunman turned, bringing his Luger around to bear on me. And my foot bumped into something hard that scuttered across the deck with a metallic clanking.

I had stopped running, involuntarily, as I watched Randy topple over the side, so my foot hadn't kicked the object far. Glancing down, I saw immediately what it was. The Luger I hadn't been able to find after I'd knocked down the first of the two gunmen. Apparently, it had slid along the deck under the rows of parked cars when he fell.

I wasted no time in idle speculation. Bending down, I scooped the automatic and straightened up. The remaining gunman, not sure what I was up to, had begun ducking down as well, possibly to loose off a shot at me underneath the cars. He was just beginning to realize his mistake and stand back up when I emerged, erect, from behind the car that blocked me from his view. In blind panic and urged on by the searing pain of loss and grief overwhelming me, I leveled the Luger and pulled the trigger four times in rapid succession. My earlier hope that I would never have to use a gun to take a man's life fleetingly receded. But the guilt I'd always imagined would deluge me into a swamp of shame never materialized. Instead I was overcome by the desire to avenge Randy's murder.

I'm no marksman, and it couldn't have been anything but blind luck that enabled me to hit him. But at least one of my shots found its mark, and possibly more. I saw his body jerk backward and crash into the tail-gate before slumping down onto the deck. Only then did my muscles begin to quiver as the reaction to all that had happened in the few brief minutes hit me.

I dropped the gun on the deck and raced for the stern. My first instinct was to dive overboard to try to save Randy, but I briskly grasped that doing so would most likely only lead to both our demises. There was a round life preserver on the bulkhead, and in a move of panic, I yanked it down and heaved it over the side. Even as I threw it, I knew it was a futile gesture at best, but something in me refused to accept that Randy was gone, and I had to give him the benefit of the doubt.

I stared back into the rainswept darkness for a few minutes, then turned and sank down onto the deck, my back against the tailgate, my knees drawn up under my chin. I wrapped my arms around my legs and began shivering violently, very little of it caused by the cold dampness of the air. I felt alone and lost—and still facing I didn't know what. Brunner, I was sure, had more henchmen where these had come from. I felt powerless to stop him from achieving his terrible scheme. Even if he didn't win the election for president, his mere announcement of who he was and what his intentions were would be enough to shake up the political structure of the country for a long time. Long enough, perhaps, that it might never totally recover.

And all I had to stop him was that damned birth certificate, hidden safely away on the roof of Randy's apartment.

Which brought me back around to Randy. The first man I had gotten serious about since Paul's death. It had been a good feeling, too. A very good feeling to finally emerge from the protective shell in which I'd encased myself. At least until this business thrust its ugly head into my life.

But I'd been convinced it was a temporary state of affairs. When it concluded, I'd thought that Randy and I would have a chance to begin building a solid, lasting relationship. Maybe I'd been deluding myself because that was what I had suddenly, desperately wanted. But now I would have no chance to find out. Brunner's henchmen had seen to that.

I sat up with a start. Brunner's henchmen! Scattered around the vehicle deck like so many rag dolls. I stood up quickly, realizing I couldn't leave them there in plain sight for the returning passengers to discover.

I checked the man who sat slumped against the tailgate to my left. There was no pulse that I could feel, nor any sign of breathing. To the best of my limited knowledge, he was dead. So, without a trace of a guilty conscience, I hoisted him up on my shoulders, being very careful not to get any blood on my clothes. He was even heavier than he looked, but eventually I managed to push and shove him up level with the top of the tailgate. With one last straining effort, I pushed him over the top, and he disappeared into the darkness and rainy gloom beyond. I didn't even hear a splash.

The second man still lay where I'd left him, and he was still unconscious. His jaw was pushed over unnaturally to one side, and I had no doubt it was fractured. His breathing was shallow and raspy, and I decided I had possibly cracked a rib or two as well when I landed on him. But he was definitely alive, and despite everything, I was no cold-blooded killer. I didn't think I could stomach dispatching *another* soul. That ruled out the same method of disposal I had used on his partner.

Carefully, I eased him into a fireman's carry. He moaned once as his chest pushed down against my shoulders, confirming my diagnosis of his ribs. But although I was no murderer, I was beyond caring about his physical comfort. Sparing no time to be gentle, I dogtrotted around several cars until I came to the nondescript sedan I had seen them emerge from. It was only then I realized they must have followed us from Victoria. There hadn't been enough time for anyone to track us up from Seattle, so they must have already been stationed on the Canadian side.

But this, too, was useless speculation, and I let it slide for later analysis. At the moment, I had a body to conceal. Glancing into the car, I noticed they hadn't taken the time to lock the doors. In fact, the keys were still protruding from the ignition.

I was about to push my unconscious burden into the back seat and hope no one noticed when I got another idea. I laid the gunman back down on the deck, opened the door of the car, and grabbed the keys. There were four others on the ring beside the car key. The car itself was a Chevrolet of fairly recent vintage, and the same key that turned the ignition also opened the trunk. I opened it quickly, hoisted the man back onto my shoulders, and dumped him unceremoniously inside. I had to bend his legs around under his chin, and I knew that when he finally regained consciousness, he would be very uncomfortable. But I didn't care. After making sure no part of his clothing was hanging out, I slammed the trunk lid down, locking it.

Going back around to the driver's door, I leaned across the seat and pushed down the lock on the passenger side. After pulling myself out of the car, I locked the driver's door as well. Then, without thinking about it, I dropped the key ring into my left-hand trouser pocket.

Moving quickly, I returned to the car Randy and I had driven aboard, grabbed the pack of cigarettes I'd originally come down for, and then closed and locked the door. Hurrying while trying to appear inconspicuous, I returned to the passenger lounge and the two half-filled cups of coffee I'd left only minutes before.

In fact, I had been gone so short a time that the coffee was still hot. Surreptitiously, I emptied the contents of Randy's cup into my own. Then, when I had determined no one was paying me inordinate attention, I took my cup and moved to an empty table nearby. That way, I figured, anyone who took notice would think I was a passenger alone. And even as I thought it, I knew paranoia was beginning to set in.

I should have gone immediately to the authorities on board the ship. It would have been the reasonable, sensible thing to do. But some niggling little voice in the back of my head kept telling me not to. And finally, as I thought it through, I could see the sense in it. If I went to the authorities, I would have to lay out in detail what Randy and I had been through. And that would mean revealing the existence of the birth certificate.

Who knew how many of these people would also become targets for Brunner's paid killers if they knew of the document's existence. I didn't want that on my conscience. But, more selfishly than that, I knew that going to the ferry's captain would involve me in more official red tape, and I was in no mood for it. Nor did I have the time. If Brunner was to be stopped, it had to be quickly. Not after a prolonged official debate and analysis.

And that was when I realized I wasn't powerless, no matter how alone. After all, I was the sole individual who knew the whereabouts of the birth certificate. I was the only one who could produce it for Brunner. And I knew that without that document, Brunner's efforts were doomed to fail—or at least suffer a seriously damaging setback.

That was also when I realized I wasn't out of it yet. I was in it now, for better or worse, until its conclusion.

I sat on the passenger deck, my nerves tautly awaiting the sounds that would signal that someone had found the unconscious man in the trunk of his car. Paranoia reared its ugly head one more time, and, rationalizing as much as I could, the feeling of being watched by everyone on board wouldn't leave me.

When I heard the announcement that all passengers with vehicles should return to the vehicle deck, I rose slowly from the table and sauntered back down below with a nonchalance I did not feel. The back of my neck burned with the glare of a thousand eyes boring into me. But no one challenged me, and no hue or cry went up.

I fully expected my car to be stopped before I got off the ferry, but the order to halt never came. Once ashore, I slowly nosed the car forward with the snail's pace of traffic. It had to be only a matter of moments, I knew, before the unattended car was found and the ferry crew realized something was wrong.

Fortunately, most of the traffic was heading due east, up the hill toward the center of town and First Hill beyond, so when I turned north onto First Avenue, I had a fairly unobstructed path ahead of me. I moved along as quickly as speed laws would allow so as not to draw unwanted attention.

Then it dawned on me that I had no idea where I was going.

19

THE LUMINOUS DIAL ON my watch showed a little after ten, matching the four hours past dinnertime that my stomach was announcing. It had been announcing for some time, in fact, but I'd been too busy and too otherwise frazzled at the nerves to pay attention. Now I suddenly found I couldn't ignore it any longer.

The rain that had started in Victoria was still sheeting outside, and a brief image of the birth certificate, wrapped in its protective plastic casing and securely fastened to the roof of Randy's apartment building, flashed through my mind. I should have been more concerned about it than I was, but my stomach's insistent demands to be pacified were driving everything else out of my brain.

I knew the symptom all too well. My nerves were wound too tight. And whenever that happened, no matter what the reason, my stomach reacted with grossly overexaggerated hunger pains.

Only this time, there was some substance to the pain. I hadn't eaten since the hasty breakfast I'd thrown together for Judy and myself early that morning. And that thought set me off thinking about Judy. I couldn't help but brood that she might be the only other living person in my life so important and dear to my heart that it would shatter whatever was left of my being if I lost her too. I was relieved to remember she was probably safe with her sister.

I parked the car on a nearly deserted First Avenue and ran for the corner, where the lights still shone in the windows of a small diner. I wasn't expecting much, but anything would be better than nothing.

The only thing on the flyspecked menu that looked at all inspiring was the special for the day: meat loaf and mashed potatoes. I ordered it, along with a large glass of milk, a tossed salad, and a piece of cherry pie with ice cream. I asked the waiter for a cup of coffee while I was waiting, lit a cigarette, and sat back to reflect on my situation.

Death was the first thing that intruded on my awareness. For the past three days, it had been following me around like a recently adopted puppy. Wrenshurst was dead. Gerhardt was dead. Brunner's two gunmen were dead. Or anyway, one was dead and the other seriously incapacitated in the trunk of his car.

And, lord, he might be dead, too, for all I knew. I hadn't thought to see if an adequate air supply could find its way into that trunk. And I had no way of knowing how long it might take someone to discover him there. If he didn't regain consciousness, no one might think to look. And if they'd succeeded in getting the engine started in order to move that car off the ferry, carbon monoxide might have finished him off. I'd read somewhere that carbon monoxide poisoning was not pleasant, no matter what anyone said.

I pulled myself up short. I was beginning to get ghoulish, and I didn't think I had the stomach for that. Especially since the waiter was setting my meat loaf in front of me.

I ate it with great relish. Not that it was particularly good, but it was filling. The potatoes were cold, and the gravy was lumpy. The peas that came with it were wrinkled and looked as if they'd cooked a week or two too long. But at that moment, I would have paid twice the price for it with gladness. By the time I got to the pie that was buried under a runny pool of what I had to assume had once been ice cream, I was almost beginning to feel human again.

Until my mind again turned to death in the way that minds sometimes unpredictably and almost uncontrollably seem to do.

And then I had to add in the cat, Oliver, as well as Randy to the death toll.

And then I didn't feel so great anymore.

I paid for my meal and ran back through the rain to the car. I'd been driving up First Avenue in the direction of Queen Anne Hill for several blocks before it hit me again that I didn't know where I was going.

I couldn't stand the thought of another First Avenue fleabag, although I would have braved it if absolutely necessary. As to anything more closely resembling a civilized hotel, well, I didn't know how many bodies Brunner could muster, but I had a sneaking hunch that I could count on one of them inhabiting the lobby of almost any decent hotel I might check in to. So, for the moment, that ruled out hotels.

My house—or what was left of it—on Lake Washington would undoubtedly be staked out. As would Randy's apartment, the bookstore, and possibly Judy Grenoble's apartment as well.

So where could I go?

At Denny, I swung the car right and headed in the general direction of Capitol Hill. Traffic was light because of the rain, and I was heading down Broadway a few minutes later, past Central Seattle Community College and a few of the other landmarks that signified Capitol Hill to me.

And then I knew where I was going.

I made a left turn on Madison Street and drove up to Sixteenth. A sharp left brought me around almost to the front door of the Seattle Gay Community Center. It was an old, rambling house set up on the side of a hill, and as I eased the car alongside the curb, I could see that a light still burned in the main entrance foyer. Ahead of me, as I stepped out of the car, I could just make out the dark bulk of Group Health Hospital.

I walked up the steps to the front door of the house, found it open, and went inside. The familiar look of it hadn't changed in the three or four years since I'd been there last. I'd come there often in my first years in Seattle, anxious to join in the Gay Liberation Movement in some way. After I started living with Paul, my attendance dropped off drastically until it just didn't seem important to me anymore. Even after Paul's death, for some reason, I never bothered to go back.

In front of me was the hall that led toward the back of the house and the huge, old-fashioned kitchen where the staff ate—and where they brewed up their frequent and fantastic vats of hot chocolate, which they dispensed liberally at their many social functions. To my left was a small living room used for information get-togethers and small, intimate discussion groups. To my right was the heart of the center's telephone counseling service. There was a huge formal dining room down the hall to the right, just behind the telephone room. Long ago, it had been converted into a formal discussion and seminar room.

The second floor contained individual counseling rooms, and the third floor contained a few tiny bedrooms where the permanent staff resided. The basement was utilized for occasional Saturday-night dances and other group social functions that required more space than was available upstairs.

A young man I'd never seen before came toward me from the telephone room. I turned to face him, trying to bring some warmth to the smile that cracked my weary face.

"Can I help you?" he asked me. "We're kind of closed."

I pointed to a chair just inside the double French doors that divided the telephone room from the entrance hall. "Can I sit down a minute?"

"Sure," the kid said. "Like I told you, we're kind of closed for the night, but I'd be glad to help you if I can."

I lit a cigarette, noticing the floor ashtray to my left. "I don't know exactly how to start this," I said, looking at him. He had clear, pale-blue eyes beneath a mop of loose, wavy brown hair. His complexion was milky smooth, and I envied him the fact that, at most, he probably only had to shave once every three days.

"You don't look all that good," he said. "Would you like a cup of coffee or something?"

I nodded, feeling fatigue wash over me like a thick, viscous wave. "Coffee would be fine. Thanks."

He left the room and came back moments later carrying two Styrofoam cups. The one he handed me was black, but I was too tired to care. I sipped at it gratefully.

The kid pulled up a chair and sat facing me. "My name's Dan," he said, holding out his hand.

I juggled the cup and my cigarette into my left hand and shook his. "Mine's Carl."

"Well, Carl, what's the problem?"

"The actual problem," I told him, "is that I need a place to catch some sleep for a while where no one will disturb me. You know, where no one would have any idea where I am."

"You're not running from the police or anything?" A frown furrowed his brow.

"I don't think I'm explaining this at all well." I started again. "But I really can't tell you very much. You either take me on faith, or I'll have to move on. But believe me, the law is not after me. It's sort of the other way around."

The telephone rang behind us. He looked at me for a long, searching moment as the phone continued to disturb the silence. Then, as if he'd reached some sort of decision, he said, "Don't go away."

He crossed the room to the small switchboard and answered the phone, settling himself into the swivel chair, his back to me. He talked for about five minutes, but his tones were so hushed that I couldn't really hear what the conversation was about. Nor did I care. I was too interested in sipping my tepid black coffee and trying to keep from falling asleep sitting up.

Dan hung his phone up, came back, and stood over me. "Another crisis successfully averted," he said, grinning. "Listen, I don't know why I'm doing this, but you look like an all-right guy to me. And you really look like you could use some sleep. Maybe after you've had some, you'd be willing to tell me what this is all about. If not, that's OK. It's your business. Anyway, there's a room upstairs I can let you use for a while. It's sort of against the rules, you know, but they do give us a little leeway around here to use our own judgment. Finish your coffee, and I'll show you up."

A few minutes later, with my coffee gone and my cigarette crushed out in the ashtray, I followed Dan up two flights of stairs and down a short hall past several closed doors to a small room at the rear of the building.

"You can hang your clothes there," he said, pointing to an old-fashioned wooden clotheshorse in the corner. "The sheets are clean, so no problem there. I get off duty at midnight, and I'll look in on you to see you're all right. Believe me, no one will know you're here."

I thanked him, I think. My eyes were growing fuzzy in the dim light. Tiredness was overwhelming me, and just looking at the warmth of the blankets on a clean bed was wiping out my resistance. He left, closing the door behind him.

I slipped out of my clothes and hung them on the clotheshorse. The sheets felt cool and comforting as I climbed into the bed. The pillow was thick and soft, and almost before I had time to appreciate it, I'd fallen asleep.

But the sleep wasn't full or deep or refreshing. It was a twisted half sleep filled with grotesque images of a little man with a small moustache, large-barreled guns pointing at my face, and the flailing arms of a young man as his body was flung back into the darkness beyond.

I felt cold and defenseless and alone. I wanted to cry out for help, but my voice kept sticking in the back of my throat. I could feel the sweat gushing from me, leaving me in a drenching pool of unpleasantness. Lights danced in front of my eyes, only to recede and reemerge in new colors and patterns. I felt as if I were falling into an endless void, a dark abyss with nothing around me for orientation. I wanted to scream, and my throat ached with my unsuccessful attempts.

And all around me I could see the lifeless face of Randy McCutcheon, police officer, secret agent—and my friend.

I don't know how long I lay there twisting and turning before I became aware I was no longer alone in the bed. But suddenly, I was aware of it. I felt the warm contact of human flesh pressed against me. At first I thought everything had been one long, terrifying nightmare and that it was Randy lying there. But then full consciousness returned to me, and I knew it had been no dream—and that the body next to mine was not Randy's.

I gave a sudden start of fright and began twisting around to find out who it was.

"It's all right," a voice said to me out of the darkness. "It's me, Dan."

"What?" I was still a little disoriented. "What are you doing here?"

I could feel his hand slipping over my shoulder and down my back. "I came in to see if you were all right. You were twisting and turning something awful. And you were crying. I just thought you could use a little human comfort, that's all. I'll leave if you want me to."

I reached up toward my face with a tentative finger, and it came away from my cheek wet and warm. Then I again felt the warmth and comfort of his body pressed close to mine. I thought momentarily of Randy's body, cold and lifeless at the bottom of the sound. And then, suddenly, I didn't care. More than anything else in the world at that moment, I wanted to be held. I wanted someone to tell me it was all right.

"No," I whispered hoarsely, "don't go. Hold me. Tight."

His arms went around me then, pulling me closer. His lean, muscular body felt soft and yielding against mine. His lips found my face and pressed against my eyelids. Then they found my mouth and sweetly held them in their embrace. Automatically, despite everything, or maybe because of it, I found myself responding.

It was good and clean and comforting. Afterward, I said, "Thank you. You'll never even be able to guess how much I needed that at this precise moment in my life."

He put his fingers to my lips to quiet me and then pulled my head down to rest against his chest. "You don't have to thank me. I needed it as much as you did. Now, go back to sleep. I think you need that more than anything else right now."

The short, curly hairs of his chest tickled my nose, and I was going to move away from them when darkness overcame me.

20

SUNLIGHT WAS STREAMING IN the window when I woke up. I was ready to believe that what had happened between me and Dan had been a part of the night's unusual dream sequence, until I rolled over and saw him standing there. He'd just picked up his shirt and was about to put it on when he saw I was awake.

"Hi, beautiful. Feeling any better?" he said.

I stretched lazily and looked at him again. He still stood there, his shirt dangling from his hand. The light played across his torso, sculpting the slender, hard muscles of his arms and shoulders and chest into a bas-relief of light and shadow. His creamy complexion extended from his face straight down to the waistband of his blue jeans. He was an incredibly lovely sight to behold upon first opening one's eyes. His brown hair hung loosely over his forehead, partly obscuring his pale-blue eyes. He grinned at me slightly self-consciously and began putting on his shirt.

"Don't," I said. "I just want to look for a few more minutes."

He hesitated for a moment and then pulled his shirt on. "I'd like that," he said simply. "But right now you've got to get up and get dressed. I'll see you downstairs. There's coffee waiting, and I think we can scrounge up some breakfast for you."

At the door, he turned and added, "I've already squared things with the director, so don't worry about anyone seeing you. Oh, and if your name is Carl *Traeger*, you had a phone call a little while ago."

The door closed behind him at about the same time that my heart found the back of my throat.

Who? How could anyone have known? It wasn't possible. Only apparently it was. And it could only be one person. Or someone who worked for him.

I glanced down at the watch on my wrist. Twenty past nine. I'd slept later than I'd have wished. But it had done me good. I felt refreshed and ready for whatever faced me. And that I was going to be faced with more than I wanted to meet, I had no doubt.

Randy's face pushed itself into my awareness as I dressed, but I gently eased it out again. I didn't have time for that just now. Remorse and sorrow would only cripple me, and I couldn't afford anything at the moment but crisp, sharp reflexes and a calm, uncluttered mind.

Grieving would have to wait.

Dan met me at the foot of the stairs with another cup of black coffee and led me into the telephone room. He introduced me to Sandy, a red-headed girl about twenty-two or twenty-three who was manning the switchboard.

"Sandy got the call about nine o'clock," Dan informed me. "She didn't have the slightest idea who it was for, but when the caller told her you had arrived during my shift, she came up and woke me."

I could feel the heat of embarrassment climbing up the back of my neck. Dan either saw it or sensed it, for he said, "Sandy's cool. She understands these things. Anyway, after she left, I put on my robe and went down to see what it was."

He handed me a slip of paper off the switchboard. The only thing on it was a telephone number. I recognized it at once. Judy Grenoble's apartment.

"Whoever it was," Dan said, "knew you were here. I don't know how, believe me. None of us told anyone. Anyway, I'm the only one who knew."

I didn't think for even a moment that Dan had called one of Brunner's henchmen. Not after the way he'd treated me. So I must have been tailed all the way from the ferry. "I know," I said, laying my hand on his shoulder and squeezing. "It's not your fault."

"Anyway," Sandy said, joining in, "the caller said you should call this number as soon as possible. That it was important."

I took a deep breath and asked, "Was the caller a man or a woman?"

Dan looked at me. "Oh, I'm sorry, didn't I tell you? It was a woman."

A woman! My heart did flip-flops at the back of my throat. Who else could it be but Judy? And why? I'd sent her off to Portland to stay with her sister just the morning before. The morning that now seemed a lifetime away.

"Can I use that telephone?" I asked, pointing to an instrument on a small table that didn't seem to be connected to the switchboard.

"Sure," Sandy said. "It's our outside line."

I scooped up the receiver and dialed the number furiously. The phone at the other end rang twice before it was answered. Whoever was there had been waiting for my call.

"Carl?" I recognized the voice, but it wasn't Judy's. "Carl, is that you?"

My heart stopped beating, and I felt the life draining out of me. The voice seemed to come from a long way away, and it sounded very mechanical, even to me. "Yes," I said. "It's me."

"Carl, please help me. What's going—"

Her voice stopped abruptly. Seconds later—endless, void seconds later—it was replaced by a man's voice. An angry, barely controlled voice.

"Traeger, I don't have time for games. And neither do you. We've got your ex-wife here. And your son. And if you ever hope to see either one of them alive again, you'll do exactly what I tell you. Are you following me?"

I nodded dully, then remembered that whoever it was couldn't see me. "Yes," I croaked, "I follow you. Are they all right?"

"You don't ask the questions now—you got that?" he growled. "But

I'll tell you. They're both all right. For now. How long they stay that way is up to you. You got me?"

I had him, all right. "What do you want me to do?"

"I want to impress on you one thing," he said. "I spent a very long, very uncomfortable six hours in the trunk of that car. So believe me, I already feel like I have a score to settle with you. One false move on your part, and I start settling it. Believe me, it won't be very pretty."

I felt the knot in my stomach tighten. If only it'd occurred to me that sparing his life on the ferry might incite far more torment than the anguish exterminating him would have fermented. I saw both Dan and Sandy staring at me anxiously. "All right," I said. "What do you want me to do?"

"I want you to go to your bookstore. Once you're there, close the place up. I don't care what you tell your employees. Tell them you're going to take inventory or something. Anyway, get rid of them. Leave the front door unlocked, and go into your office. Then, sit there and wait. I'll be in touch with you. You have one hour."

The line went dead.

Dan looked at me, questioning. "You have to leave, don't you?"

I nodded.

"Can you tell me about it? Maybe I can help."

"No, but thanks," I said. "For everything."

He looked slightly hurt then, but it disappeared as quickly as I saw it. "Will you come back and see me?"

I looked at him, my heart going out to this boy I hardly knew. Something that seemed to be happening to me a lot recently. I thought Judy Grenoble would approve of the fact that my shell seemed to have been permanently breached. "I'll come back and see you. That's a promise." Then, ignoring Sandy's presence, I kissed him lightly on the cheek. "Take care."

I left them there, not able to look at either of them as I went. The car was where I had left it, so I got in and drove away.

As I zoomed the streets to the bookstore, my mind couldn't stop agonizing over Margaret and Eric. Although it would be wiser to follow Brunner's orders, I impulsively hatched a change of plans. Giving in to my temptation without thinking, I took a sharp U-turn, heading directly to Judy's apartment. I had to at least try to rescue them, even though the cards were stacked against me.

Arriving at Judy's apartment, I sprang out of my car, raced to her unit, and approached the backside of the building. I climbed the fire escape stairs, burst the rear window open, and immediately aimed for my family. I thought if I quietly untied them, maybe I wouldn't get spotted. I strode into the main room and espied them fastened to a couple of dining room chairs.

"I've never been happier to see you, Carl," Margaret blurted out, crying.

"Dad! Please help us!" Eric said in obvious fear.

Tears instantaneously leaked from my eyes and trickled down my cheeks. But before I had a chance to take another step, I was caught from behind and forced into an armlock. I tried to fight it and release myself, but he only applied more pressure, clamping his grip, rendering me suspended and screeching with pain.

"Nice try, Traeger. We anticipated you might try to save your family. And now you're coming with me."

I was throbbing as he adjusted the compression of his constraint on my arm. While Margaret and Eric wailed in the apartment, he pushed me outside and slammed the front door behind him. He tied my hands behind my back, shoved me into the back seat of my car, and drove us to the bookstore. I was frustrated and irate that I had failed to rescue them. Regretfully, I realized I should have devised a better plan before driving to Judy's, but I'd been too struck with emotion.

He parked my car out of sight behind a neighboring building, escorted me out of the car, and commanded I go into the bookstore and do as I had originally been told.

The girls were marvelously cooperative. They didn't question me when I told them they could have the day off with pay, that I had some things to do and didn't want to bother with having the store open. I thanked them all for looking after things and then shooed them on their way.

With the sharp pain in my arm slowly subsiding, I couldn't have been in my office more than ten seconds when the phone rang. I snatched it up and pressed it hard against my ear.

"Traeger. Don't say anything. Just listen. I don't blame you for trying to save your family. If the roles were reversed, I probably would have done the same thing. Aside from that, so far you've done good. I think it goes without saying that we don't want the police brought in on this, doesn't it? So I'm going to let you sit there for a while. When I'm satisfied no one is watching the place, I'll call you again."

"What about—" But the line was already dead.

I lit a cigarette and sat behind the desk. Looking up at the door, I could almost imagine Randy walking in, but again I gently pushed his image away. It wasn't time for that. Considering everything, it might never be time for that again.

I waited there for over an hour, my nerves stretched taut. I couldn't concentrate on the papers on my desk. I made some coffee, but it tasted bitter. I left the cup untouched, and it grew cold.

By the time the phone rang, my nerves were so strung out that I actually jumped. Grabbing the receiver, I said, "Hello! Hello? Look, whoever you are, what do you want me to do? Just tell me, and I'll do it. I give up. I've had enough."

"Easy does it, Traeger." It was the same snarling voice that had called me before. "Any minute now, you'll hear the front door of your store open. When you do, tell me."

He was quiet then, but the line remained open. I strained my ears, listening. Finally, I heard it—the faint scratching sound of the door latch scraping over the latch plate.

"OK," I said.

"Fine," he replied. "Now, call out to him and tell him you're in the back, alone and unarmed."

I did what I was told. I could hear cautious footsteps making their way across the floor beyond my office door. Then, slowly, the knob began to turn, and the door eased open, slowly, toward me.

"The office door is opening," I said, aware that I was whispering.

"Fine," he said. "It will just be a moment."

The door swung all the way open, and I stood there facing him. I'd never seen him before, but I knew instantly who it had to be. Brunner.

"You look shocked," he said.

I couldn't say anything. His face was almost delicate. He had fine brown hair that hung limply over his forehead above light-brown eyes. A thin pencil moustache graced his upper lip. He had almost no chin. He was wearing a very expensive dark-blue suit with a matching vest. His tie was deep-blue silk. I had no doubt that the stone in his tiepin was a genuine diamond, despite its overlarge size.

"You've guessed who I am, of course." It wasn't a question, merely a statement of fact. The voice was the same I'd heard on the telephone what seemed so long ago.

I nodded affirmatively.

His hand came up holding a small semiautomatic pistol. The handgrips looked like pearl, and they probably were. "Set the phone down on the desk and move back toward the wall," he said quietly.

Again, I did what I was told.

He moved over to the desk and picked up the phone. "It's all right," he said into the mouthpiece, never taking his eyes off me. "I'll take it from here. You know what to do if you don't hear from me."

I felt a cold chill go through me when I heard that. I had a pretty good idea what he meant. He hung up the phone and motioned toward my desk with the pistol. "Sit down there."

He backed away from me as I returned to my desk, taking no chances. I sat down in the chair and rolled it up under the desk so I would have to push it backward if I wanted to stand back up. I was taking no chances either.

"Now, I think we need to talk," he said.

I tried to sound cooperative. "Anything you say."

"First, let me say that you've shown far more resourcefulness and far more obstinacy than I would have expected from someone like you. Frankly, I'm rather impressed."

"What do you mean, someone like me?" I asked.

"You know," he said, "someone on the pink list. A fag. A fairy. A homo. Not known for being all that tough, if you know what I mean."

I shook my head. "Appearances can be deceiving."

"So I've found out." He chuckled at that, almost sounding amused. "Now then, where is the document? And I want no more delays. No more tricks. If there are, your ex-wife will die. And it won't be quickly, and it won't be pleasant." He paused to let it sink in. "And your son will be forced to watch."

I recoiled physically from his words, as though I'd been slapped in the face. Eric was only ten years old. Already, he must be half-terrified out of his mind. If he were forced to witness the horror Brunner was hinting at, he would probably never know another moment of sense as long as he lived.

"You win," I said dryly. I didn't feel very proud of myself, betraying all those who had already died to keep the birth certificate out of Brunner's hands, but I didn't see much choice. Even knowing what potential horror might be unleashed on the country once he had the document in his hands, I couldn't bring myself to subject Eric or Margaret to the agony that awaited them if I refused. "But unless you want a lot of curious onlookers, we'll have to wait until after dark. Preferably late tonight."

He took a step forward, waving the pistol in my direction. "You're stalling again," he said. His eyes had gone wild, staring through me like spikes. "I warned you what would happen."

"No, I'm not," I said desperately. "Listen to me."

Quickly, I explained how and where I'd hidden the birth certificate. He looked at me as if he didn't believe a word I was saying, but when I'd finished, he stepped forward another few inches and said, "Very clever. Very resourceful. Too bad you couldn't have been on my side. I could use some imagination like that. Instead, I have…" He waved the pistol around, shrugging. "Oh well, you already know what kind of people I have working for me. All right then, we'll wait. But tonight we will go. And if you are lying to me, you will watch your son watch his mother be torn apart piece by piece. Inch by inch. Think about that."

I didn't have to think about it. Just hearing him say it brought bile to my throat. This man was a cold, unfeeling monster. A sadistic brute. And I was ready to allow him access to the highest office in the land. I felt a cold wave of revulsion run through me. Revulsion at my own weakness. But I didn't change my mind.

Brunner made a phone call explaining to the man who was holding my wife and son why there was going to be a delay. He asked for a squad of men to join us at ten o'clock.

Putting the phone down, he said, "It's going to be a long wait. I have men outside watching the building. Don't try anything cute. I don't have to remind you—"

"I know, I know," I shouted at him. "You don't have to keep saying it. I'm going to do just what you ask. OK?"

The day stretched on interminably. I ran out of cigarettes just before three, and by four I was becoming edgy and irritable. And I was hungry.

"Do you think one of your goons could bring some cigarettes in here?" I asked. "And maybe some food?"

"Discipline, Mr. Traeger. Discipline," he said. "It's good for the soul.

And furthermore, smoking is such a filthy habit. Maybe after we have recovered the document. We'll see. Right now, I'd rather no one is seen coming and going from your store. It is closed, if you remember. I don't want anyone getting curious."

By ten o'clock, I was a nervous wreck. My stomach was making growling noises, and I had a curious lightheaded feeling, which I recognized as the first stages of nicotine withdrawal. I know it's nothing like withdrawing from heroin, but if you've ever gone through it, you'll know that it's damned uncomfortable. I felt like clawing my way through the wall, and if Brunner was in my way when I started, so much the better.

But I didn't. I sat there and waited, suffering in silence.

The whole time, Brunner stood quietly, occasionally consulting his watch. He didn't fidget; he didn't pace. Once, he sat down in the other chair for about half an hour, but then he resumed his standing position. His eyes and his gun never left my general direction. I didn't know if he was always that self-controlled or if it was an exhibition for my benefit. Either way, I was suitably impressed.

At ten o'clock precisely, Brunner marched me to the front door. All the lights were out in the store, and the interior was pitch black except for the dim light spilling in from the streetlamp outside. A light knock came at the door, and Brunner told me to open it. On the other side was the man who had stood in my office so long ago waving a gun in my face.

"Ah, Mr. Traeger. We meet again. You have caused me some embarrassment with my colleagues, you know. But no more, I think. Now you will give us what we want, eh?"

I said nothing. Brunner prodded me from behind, and I stepped through the door. There was a large dark van parked at the curb in front of the store. We walked across the sidewalk to it. The front had two bucket seats. Behind them, two more bench-type seats looked capable of holding three persons apiece. The man who had knocked on the door pulled open the sliding side door on the van and indicated I should get in. Brunner climbed in next to me. The door was shut quickly, and the other man slipped into the passenger seat in front. Another man was already at the wheel, three more on the seat behind us.

"Back to the apartment," Brunner told the driver.

Without saying a word, the driver eased the van into gear and pulled away from the curb. No one said anything all the way out of downtown and up the Counterbalance to the top of Queen Anne Hill. The driver pulled the van into the parking lot behind the apartment building.

Still without making a sound, the men disembarked from the van, the three behind us going out the rear doors. Brunner stood next to me, idly holding his pistol as if he no longer considered me a serious threat. I no longer felt like much of a serious threat.

"We will go inside," Brunner said, "and you will show us where the document is. Again, I repeat myself: any tricks, and you know the consequences."

Now a thoroughly cowed and shattered man, I led the way. At the back door to the apartment, Brunner stopped me. "I will be waiting here with three of my men. These two will accompany you inside. I will wait ten minutes, no more. If you aren't back by then…" He shrugged, as if he couldn't be blamed for what might happen then.

I nodded grimly, and the three of us went inside. The stairs to the basement were to our left, the stairs to the first-floor landing to our right. One of them started up in front of me. I had just placed my right foot on the stairs when two shots rang out behind us in the parking lot. The man in front of me whirled around, and I turned to face the parking lot myself. As I did, I heard a scuffling noise behind me. Then a body brushed past me and thumped heavily onto the floor next to my feet. The man who'd been behind me as we'd started up the stairs was standing at the back door with his hand on the doorknob. He turned to see what the problem was, and a shadow flitted out of the stairwell from the basement. Two seconds later, the second gunman lay on the floor by the first.

I was shocked and confused. And frightened. A lot of thoughts began crowding my mind at the same time. Among them was the realization that I'd just been rescued.

Also among them was the fact that someone had just condemned Margaret to a slow, horrible death. With Eric as the prime spectator.

Someone behind me said, "Are you all right, Mr. Traeger?"

"Yeah, fine." I nodded my head in the darkness. "Just bloody well fine."

Two officers guided me into the parking lot. Several bodies lay motionless on the ground in front of me. Several others stood with their hands on their heads. There seemed to be a dozen policemen wandering around the lot. None of it made any sense.

"Well, how you doing, guy?" someone said on my left.

I turned to look at him. The face I saw staring back at me was Randy McCutcheon's.

21

E WERE SITTING IN Randy's apartment. Someone had put a drink in my hand, and I was taking large, unchecked swallows, trying to calm myself. I'd already explained to one of the policemen where the birth certificate was, and he was now up on the roof retrieving it.

I looked to my left at Randy, who was sitting on the sofa next to me. "I thought you were dead," I said again. "I really thought you were dead."

"I almost was. In fact, if you hadn't thrown that life preserver, I probably would be. I almost didn't make it that far." He grinned at me. "I'm assuming it was you who threw it and not one of those cheap gunsels."

"Yeah," I said, swallowing some more of the liquor. "It was me. But I saw him shoot you," I persisted, my mind still unable to comprehend the difference between the reality before me and the reality my brain had constructed from what I had observed.

"Oh, he shot me all right," Randy said. "My shoulder is going to be very sore for a very long time. As for the rest, when I saw he was going to fire, I tried to twist out of his way. I didn't quite make it, as the doctor can attest. Anyway, as I twisted, I slipped in the puddle of water that was covering the deck. My own movement and the natural movement of the ferry did the rest. My feet went out from under me, and over the side I went."

He grinned again. "Actually, it probably saved my life. If I'd fallen on the deck, he would have had plenty of time for a second shot. And at that range, I don't think he would have missed."

He took my glass and refilled it from the bottle on the coffee table. I was slightly taken aback and dispirited that Randy hadn't kissed or embraced me yet, but I figured there'd be a more appropriate time for that. Handing the glass back to me, he said, "I was lucky. A fishing boat came by about half an hour later and picked me up. I was unconscious when they hoisted me, but once I came to, I used their radio and called ahead to the police. I asked them to stake out places where you most likely would have gone, including my apartment and the bookstore.

"Oh, and by the way, Sergeant Yates asked me to tell you how grateful he is that we didn't damage his car."

"Tell the sergeant I'm happy to have obliged him," I said bitterly. "You realize, don't you, that you've condemned my ex-wife to a slow, agonizing death? And probably my son as well? You realize that, right?" My voice had risen to a shrill, near-hysterical shout. "But good God, by all means, tell Sergeant Yates I'm thrilled beyond words that nothing happened to his car."

Randy stared at me steadily. "They're all right, Carl."

I stopped shouting and blinked at him stupidly. "What?"

"I said they're all right. We were tipped off as to their whereabouts and took Judy Grenoble's apartment without firing a shot right after Brunner left the bookstore with you."

"You're telling me the truth?" I stared at him, not ready to trust the emotions I was feeling.

"They're a little shaken up, but otherwise they're all right," he repeated. "You'll see them down at the station in a few minutes."

"And Brunner?" I asked. "What about Brunner?"

"He's dead. He took a shot at us when we told them to drop their weapons. I shot back. Believe me, he's very, very dead. It's all over, Carl."

"All over?" I repeated mechanically. I found it quite unfathomable that after all that had transpired, the head honcho of this entire plight was suddenly bereft of life. That despite all the menacing incidents he'd left in his wake, which had surely seemed like deadlocks at the time, his operation had so swimmingly expired—and with it, the objective of his life's work.

"Well, almost," Randy said. "We've still got to go up to Kodiak and pick up old Horst. Brunner's father. But that shouldn't be too difficult. He's just an old man."

"Well, have a good time," I said, feeling weary beyond my years.

"You mean you're not going with me?" He grinned at me again, and despite myself, I grinned back. "You've seen it through this far, you know. And none of these guys"—he waved his arm around, indicating the Seattle police officers who were wandering around the room—"have any jurisdiction up there." He stared at me intently. "What do you say? You want to see how it all ends, don't you?"

The damned thing was that I did. And he knew it. I nodded in acquiescence.

"Good," he said, grinning again. "We'll leave first thing in the morning."

And we did just that. After I'd seen my ex-wife and my son for a very emotional, very strained reunion. I talked with them for a long time, much of it spent reacquainting myself with a little boy I hadn't seen in far too long. Before they left, I promised Margaret I would do better at keeping in touch. I promised Eric I would write to him and that I'd come visit him as soon as his summer vacation began. I wasn't sure how Margaret felt about that, but she agreed to it. It seemed to make Eric happy too. And for some reason, I felt pretty good about it myself. Better than I'd felt about my ex-wife in a long time.

Randy assured me they would be under police protection while traveling to the airport and that the Ohio State Police would keep them under close surveillance until they were sure any threat was gone. I had no choice but to trust him, so I left it in their hands.

Kodiak looked very much as it had when I'd left it at the end of my hitch in the navy. Randy had found out for me that the navy pulled out of Kodiak in the early seventies, leaving the base to the Coast Guard. Beyond that, very little had changed on the island. There were still more bars than churches, and the fishermen still brought in the largest, best king crab anywhere in the world.

The plane settled into the approach pattern, dipped down toward the runway, and sailed in over the road that twisted from the old navy base into the town of Kodiak proper. It was the only airport I'd ever seen where stoplights brought traffic to a halt so planes could safely land on the runway without ripping through the side of a jeep or a truck. But then, I supposed the residents of Kodiak were grateful they even had an airport capable of handling a 707. They'd be pretty inaccessible otherwise.

We rented a car at the airport, drove out to the base road, turned right, and headed toward the town. The old ship-turned-cannery flashed past on our right as we rounded the curve that brought us into view of the row of canneries leading like stepping stones down the shoreline into Kodiak. Up to our left, dotting the hill and well hidden by trees and undergrowth, were the old bunkers that had once formed part of the defense perimeter during the Second World War. I remembered going up and exploring them one afternoon the last time I'd been there.

It seemed strange to me that the whole year I'd served in Kodiak, I'd been less than ten miles away from an old man who might be Adolf Hitler. It was a mind-boggling thought.

"Doesn't it scare you a little?" I asked Randy. I was driving, by virtue of the fact that I'd been there before. Randy was leaning against the passenger door, smoking a cigarette and staring out across the water of the bay near Old Women's Mountain. Out in the water, I could see the large rock with the natural arch in the middle that my chief had once flown me over in the base air club's old World War II training plane.

Randy turned to me. "Doesn't what scare me?"

"You know. Meeting Hitler face to face. Or, at least, doesn't it give you a chilly kind of feeling?"

"Yeah, a little," he said.

"Don't you think we should have brought someone else along with us?"

He shook his head. "I told you. He's an old man. His son is dead. His plan is shattered. I've got the birth certificate right here." He patted his jacket pocket, where I could see the edge of the folded document protruding. Randy planned on using it to persuade the old man to come along quietly. "When we get him back to Washington, someone who's clever enough to sort these things out will sort this thing out. I'm no philosopher, nor am I a diplomat. I'm just a policeman."

He turned back to look across the water. "I don't think he's going to give us any trouble. But if he does, I have this." His fingers touched his jacket where it covered the waistband of his slacks—where his revolver lay hidden in his belt holster.

We drove into town, passing the old Russian Orthodox church on our right. The town square was situated on the next block, containing most of the stores and taverns. We drove past that, and past the movie theater in the next block as well. The tall masts of the fishing fleet were already behind us. About two miles past the center of the town, we made a left-hand turn onto an old dirt road and followed it about a quarter mile to the end. A small house sat there, half-hidden by the tall evergreens that surrounded it.

We parked the car and walked up to the front door. There was no doorbell, so Randy knocked. We waited a few minutes, but no one answered. He knocked again. Still no answer.

"So now what do we do?" I asked, feeling let down. We'd come all this way, apparently for nothing.

"We'll go back to the car and wait awhile," Randy said.

"You will both put your hands above your heads," a voice behind us said. "Don't turn around. Don't move. Just put your arms up."

I didn't wait for a second invitation. My arms shot upward like twin rockets launching from Cape Canaveral. I could feel the joint in my right shoulder pop in protest. Next to me, a little slower, Randy followed suit.

"Now then, you on the right," the voice behind us continued. "You will lower your left arm very slowly to open the door, then put your arms back up and walk into the house. I have a gun lined up on your backs. A shotgun, loaded with elk cartridges. At this range, it would slice you in half. I suggest you make no sudden or stupid moves. Once you are inside, you will take four paces into the center of the room and stop. You will keep your hands in the air."

I was the one on the right. I lowered my left arm so slowly I thought old age was going to set in. Carefully, I opened the door. It swung back on squeaky hinges. I stepped into the room and took four paces to the center, then stopped, keeping my arms up in plain sight. I felt more than saw Randy move in behind me and stop at my side.

There was a slight noise behind us and then the sound of the door closing. I heard what sounded like a bolt sliding home.

"Now," the voice said calmly, "you will turn around slowly."

I didn't argue. Slowly, I turned toward Randy as he was turning toward me, his face expressionless. We completed our semicircle and stood facing our captor. For the first time, we could see who it was.

I wanted to faint and throw up at the same time. The man standing there aiming the shotgun at us was John Brunner.

"You're dead," I heard myself saying.

"On the contrary," he said. "I'm very much alive." "But you can't be," Randy protested. "I shot you myself. And believe me—you were very, very dead."

He snorted in amusement. "I'm sure whoever you shot is very dead,

Mr. McCutcheon. Or, should I say, Officer McCutcheon. And since you are convinced that it had to be me, I can only assume that the man you claim to have killed was my twin brother, Johann."

I heard myself gasping again. "Your twin brother?"

"You mean Adolf Hitler had twins?" Randy asked, clearly as flabbergasted as I was.

Brunner laughed again. "I'm not sure that Adolf Hitler ever had any children. If the truth be known, I suspect the crazy old fool was sterile. But that, of course, is just between you and me."

"Of course," Randy said, beginning to recover his wits. "But, if you'll pardon me, I don't exactly understand. We've been laboring under the impression that Adolf Hitler had a twin brother who died in his place in the bunker, while the real Adolf escaped to Canada."

"A useful story, don't you think?" Brunner said. "And quite a few people believe it, too. Which is exactly what my father had in mind when he created it."

I stood there feeling very numb. "I don't understand at all," I said. "Maybe I'm stupid, but I don't understand at all."

"Easy enough to understand, actually," he said. "You would be Traeger, am I right? The description matches."

I nodded.

"Well then, Mr. Traeger, I will explain it to you. You see, at the end of the war, my father realized Adolf Hitler's dream was going down the drain, so to speak. He had no heirs. His heir adoptive, Martin Bormann, had disappeared off the face of the earth. But my father wasn't content to see that happen. So he gathered several trusted friends around him and told them of a plan that could mean the reemergence of the Reich at a later, more opportune time. Your uncle was one of those men. Gerhardt was another. They forged the birth certificate for use at a later time and then hid it in the book. Your uncle was charged with bringing it out of

Germany. Gerhardt was charged with removing his vast wealth and setting it up in Canada to finance the plan when it was ready to bloom.

"The only thing we didn't count on was losing the birth certificate. Your uncle died before he could tell us where he had hidden it."

A fanatical gaze was spreading over his eyes, but his grip on the shotgun never faltered.

"So when we discovered you were in line to inherit, we made a few alterations in the plan. We decided to use you to give credibility to the document."

"I don't follow," I said, puzzled.

"It's really quite simple. If we had merely recovered the document after all these years, there would have been too many who would be skeptical. So, instead, we allowed a few words to be leaked out. Mr. McCutcheon's department took the bait. When you obtained the document, we began chasing you for it, not even intending to recover it in the beginning. The theory was that we would not expend so much energy and so many lives trying to recover a fake. As it stands now, there are people in Washington who are at least ninety percent sure that the birth certificate is genuine. Isn't that true, Officer McCutcheon?"

Randy's face was a dark mask of anger. He'd been used as well, and I could tell he didn't like it. "It's true," he said between clenched teeth.

"Then, I'm afraid," Brunner went on, "you showed a little too much ingenuity, and we lost track of it. That was when we began playing the game in earnest. We would have had your ex-wife for leverage much sooner, but she remarried somewhere along the way, and it took us a considerable amount of time and trouble to locate her."

It felt as if someone had slammed a fist into my stomach. I hadn't known about Margaret's remarriage. Even though we'd been divorced for a considerably long time, and even though I no longer loved her—if I indeed ever had—it came as quite a shock.

Brunner must have seen it on my face. "I'm sorry, Mr. Traeger. I thought you knew that. Ah, well, rest assured. Her second husband left her about a year ago. Why she persisted in using his name is beyond me. But no matter. I am led to believe my incompetent brother bungled even that. Perhaps it is just as well. It would never have done any good to keep him around anyway. So, Mr. McCutcheon, I suppose I should thank you for performing a rather unpleasant task for me."

The coldness of it, the callousness, did more to convince me what kind of man we were facing than any ten shotguns could have. And I knew then that neither Randy nor I would leave that room alive.

"But all is well now," Brunner said. "My secret is safe in this room. The document has been returned to me, and the plan will go on as before." He pointed at Randy's jacket pocket. "I presume that the piece of paper sticking out of your pocket is the certificate?"

"It is," Randy said.

"If you would be so kind," Brunner instructed, "take it out of your pocket with your thumb and forefinger, and lay it there on that table."

Brunner backed out of striking range of the table as Randy plucked the document out of his coat pocket. He walked to the table, but instead of setting it down, he unfolded it and held it up in front of him. He did it so quickly that I realized it wasn't spontaneous. He'd planned on doing it before he'd taken the first step. For the life of me, I couldn't understand what he hoped to gain by it. I didn't have to wait very long to find out.

Randy's sudden movement caught Brunner off guard as well. "What do you think you're doing?" he demanded.

"I think we have a stalemate here," Randy said. "If you pull the trigger, you will undoubtedly succeed in blowing me to bits. *But*—and this is a very long but—you will also succeed in blowing this piece of paper to a thousand pieces. I don't think you want that. So I don't think you will risk shooting."

"But I will," a voice said. It was a female voice, coming from behind us, to our left.

And it was a voice I found chillingly familiar.

We both turned to look at the same time. There, standing in the doorway that presumably led to the bedrooms, with a slim, pearl-handled automatic surprisingly like John Brunner's in her hand, was Judy Grenoble.

I was past the point of anything else shocking my nervous system by then. I merely stared at her in complete noncomprehension.

"You would be the sister, then," Randy said calmly.

"You knew?" I blurted out.

"We suspected," Randy answered. "We only got confirmation last night."

"As I said," she repeated, "I will shoot. And most willingly. Nor will my bullet do any damage to the document. So unless you want to die standing there, you will do as my brother asks and place the piece of paper on the table."

Randy didn't move.

"I trusted you!" I screamed at Judy.

She turned her attention to me for the first time. "That was the easiest part of all," she said. "Your Paul fell for it so quickly. So eager to be flattered. And with no danger to me of ever having to prove what he thought I felt for him.

"And *you*," she spat. "You were like putty in my hands. So ready to be comforted. So easily led. That night in my apartment, I wanted to claw your eyes out. But it was not yet time. So I allowed you to send me on my way."

"But your sister in Portland," I stammered.

"One of ours. Do you think we lacked planning? Do you think I just chanced to show up for employment at your store? We worked very hard to make sure I was better qualified than anyone else. You hired me because we left you no choice."

All the pieces seemed to be falling neatly into place. Of course she had suggested I tell Randy about the birth certificate—Brunner had just finished telling us they'd wanted official verification of the document's genuineness. And they must have already known Randy was more than he seemed to be. Which meant that there was a rather high-level leak in Randy's organization. I glanced at him and could see he had just worked out as much for himself.

It also occurred to me that Brunner's men hadn't needed to keep close tabs on us a great deal of the time. Judy would have been able to tell them right where we were. At least when we went up to his apartment. Or when I came to her apartment that night.

I felt pretty foolish now, thinking about it.

She turned away from me and looked back at Randy. "Now," she said, "do as I tell you, and set that document on the table, or I will shoot you where you stand."

Randy hesitated, looking at me and then down at the floor.

"At once," she screamed, and I had the feeling that shooting another human being, face to face, was something alien to her. I might have imagined it, but I thought I'd heard a faint tremor in her voice. Had it been anger or uncertainty?

"Of course," Randy said.

He turned back toward the table and stretched out his arm. Just as I thought he was going to lay the paper down, he snapped his wrist and sent the birth certificate sailing in Brunner's direction. At the same time, he launched himself sideways, his right hand clawing at the gun still hidden beneath his jacket.

The moment I saw him move sideways, I dropped to the floor. And not a moment too soon. Randy's sudden movement caught Brunner off guard. He had been paying too much attention to his sister. The fraction of a second it took him to recover his sense cost him his life.

His shotgun went off with an ear-shattering blast. I could feel a piece of shot tearing through my hair as I dropped. Behind me, I heard a bloodcurdling scream.

Randy's hand came out from under his jacket filled with cold, black steel. Two spurts of flame shot from the barrel, and Brunner doubled up and collapsed on the floor. The air stank of cordite, and my ears were still ringing from the shotgun blast. Slowly, shakily, I got back to my feet.

I already had a good idea what I would find behind me, and I almost couldn't force myself to turn around for confirmation. But I knew I had to. I owed her that much. Although, for the life of me, I couldn't have explained why.

I hadn't expected it to be quite so messy. The shotgun blast had caught her along the right side of the head, tearing away her ear, a good deal of hair, and most of the right side of her jaw. I suppose it would be hard to say whether it was the shock or the massive loss of blood that killed her. Either way, she was very, very dead.

I turned back to Randy, who was just standing up over Brunner's prone figure. "He's dead," he said simply.

"And the birth certificate?"

He picked up a few tiny scraps of paper off the table. "I think the shotgun took care of that also."

I nodded my head dumbly.

"I suppose we ought to see what's in the bedroom," he said, starting for the door.

I could find no arguments against it, so I followed him, carefully stepping around Judy's mutilated body.

Inside the room we found an old man tucked into an enormous bed, the blankets pulled clear up to his chin. The only thing visible was his head. His hair was nearly all gone, and what was left of it was a dirty yellow-white, plastered to his gray-pink skull. His watery eyes had a faraway, unfocused look. A thin line of spittle ran down from the corner of his mouth across his cheek. In spite of learning that Adolf Hitler wasn't really Brunner's father, the possibility had still been frightening. But this image confirmed Brunner's assertion that it was clearly someone else.

"That television's too loud!" he shrilled. "Have you come to bring me my dinner?"

It was as obvious a case of senility as could have been witnessed. He stared straight at us and never saw us at all. I didn't think anyone would ever know what was going on inside his head.

"Horst Brunner?" I asked quietly.

"It must be," Randy agreed.

"What do we do with him?" I asked. So badly, I wanted the whole thing to be over with.

"I hate to ask you," Randy said, "but one of us has to stay here while the other goes and fetches the police. I think that will have to be you. They'll believe a fellow police officer a heck of a lot faster than they will a civilian."

I nodded, agreeing with his logic.

At the front door, he turned to me. "You going to be all right?"

"I'm fine," I said.

"I won't be long." He punched me gently on the shoulder, and then he was out the door and into the car.

I stood there for a long time, watching the car disappear down the dirt road. And I stood there a long time after it was gone, unable to turn around and face what lay behind me.

22

Two days later, I stood in the living room of my house on Lake Washington. I'd come to look at it for the last time before putting it up for sale. It seemed like a totally alien place now, as far removed from me as the man I had been two weeks before.

So little objective time had passed since my trip back to Philadelphia to straighten out Aunt Sophie's will. Yet so many years of subjective time had elapsed. I felt so much older. And so much wiser? Possibly. Having been faced with death and teased with close encounters of it, I now felt my mortality on a whole other, extraordinary level. I realized every day that passed by wasn't coming back. We were all only inching up to our departure with each dawn to dusk that slipped away. Avoiding risks was more desirable, but the past two weeks had taught me it didn't always pay to play it safe.

With that in mind, before long I had mailed a check and gave away the fortune I'd inherited to the Leukemia Society of America in Paul's honor. Up until this point, I hadn't conceived that it was keeping me from fully living my life just as much as the shell I'd needed to come out of. Inherent to the desire was the source of its fulfillment.

Randy had apologized for the extensive debriefing I'd had to go through, but it was important to senior members of his agency that everything was recorded—minutely, accurately, and before any of it had time to become fogged in my memory. I'd gone through it mechanically, steered by the fact that once it was over, I would be free of it.

Strangely, after I'd left the office, I had felt free of it, as if it had all happened to someone else.

My last hour with Randy had come as no great surprise to me either. He was forthright about his intentions. It was disenchanting to hear and disheartening to come to terms with, to say the least.

"I thought I was in love with you, you know that?" I said to him.

"I keep hoping that maybe you were," he said, unable to look at me.

"I feel so used. I thought you loved me too."

He looked at me then. "You're very special to me, Carl. I hope you'll always remember that. I felt very deeply toward you. And I know there's no way to apologize to you for playing with your emotions. But I had to be close to you. You must see that?"

"Oh, I see it," I said. "And I understand it. But understanding it doesn't make it feel any better."

"Just remember this," he said. "I came closer to loving you than I ever have with anyone before. Believe that. Please.

"But I could never allow myself to fall in love with you or anyone else. Even more, I could never allow you to fall in love with me. Look at me—I'm a killer. I'm an agent. It's what I do, and I do it well. I could never give it up, and I could never ask you to become involved with it. I'm sorry."

"I understand," I said flatly. I'd been half expecting it since I'd first seen him alive outside his apartment building after thinking he'd died going over the side of the ferry. He hadn't kissed me once. He hadn't touched me affectionately. He hadn't indicated in any way that things were the same between us, as I'd thought they were.

I'd wanted to believe it was the expediency of the moment, that he was so close to wrapping up the case that his mind was on other things.

But I guess deep down I'd known what he was going to tell me before he did. I just hadn't really wanted to hear it.

He gave my arm an affectionate punch before he left, and I never saw him again.

Now, standing in my living room, looking at the loose plaster on the floor and the gaping holes in the walls, it all seemed so distant. I knew I wasn't going to have too much difficulty putting it behind me. And this time, I didn't think I'd be constructing any shell of self-pity to hide behind.

I looked over at the front door as I became aware of a persistent scratching sound. I looked from the door to where Dan was standing across the room. He looked back at me and shook his head. His pale-blue eyes were alive with life and excitement, and I was very glad I'd kept my promise to go back and see him.

Shrugging, I turned back to the door and went to open it. As it swung into the living room, I looked down and saw the familiar orange shape of an old friend crossing the threshold.

It was Paul's cat, Oliver. I would have recognized him anywhere. He looked up at me in his accusatory way, as if it to complain at the shabby treatment he'd received for the last several days with no one around to feed him.

I didn't know by what miracle he'd escaped his intended fate and some other poor cat had been forced into his place, and I didn't care. I reached down and scooped him off the floor, cradling him in my arms, pressing my face against his. He struggled once to free himself from my embrace and then settled down, resigned to accepting it.

Suddenly, I started laughing. Uncontrollably. Despite everything that had happened, I knew that I was going to be all right. I knew life was going to be all right from here on out.

Randy had told me Brunner's contacts in Washington were being carefully investigated, and it would only be a matter of time before his entire organization was broken. Democracy would be safe once again.

Until the next threat.

But all that was far away from me. It had nothing to do with me. I was out of it.

Dan walked across the room and stood beside me. His eyes looked anxious. "Is everything all right?"

I looked at him through streaming tears. Then I wrapped my arm around his waist and pulled him close. The cat was cradled in the crook of my other arm, nonchalantly licking his foot.

"Everything is fine," I told him.

Then I started laughing again.

Special thanks to Kira Wolak and Allison Erin Wright for inspiration.

CPSIA information can be obtained
at www.ICGtesting.com
Printed in the USA
LVHW091052060119
602918LV00012B/163/P